COLD WATER FOREST

FREDRICK NILES

FEVER GARDEN PUBLISHING

COLD WATER FOREST

First edition. December 1, 2021.

ISBN: 978-1-950021-11-6

Fever Garden Publishing

Cover design by

TheCoverCollection.com

❀ Created with Vellum

"Civilizations are the summer noise of
insects between two winters."

— Nicolás Gómez Dávila

1

———

WE DROVE DEEP INTO THE BLACKENED FOOTHILLS, THE PALE road squirming out ahead of us like a thin worm. The night was matte black and starless, the crescent moon overhead so thin it was barely there at all. Shapes would occasionally dart out in front of the car, eyes streaking over the gravel like pairs of bouncing yellow fireflies set with the hunched and ragged features of a weasel or some other nocturnal varmint.

My daughter, Haylie, sat silently behind me, her eyes drinking in the bleak autumn landscape as it rolled by through the window. She was eleven. Quiet for her age with her father's long black hair and narrow cheekbones.

In the passenger seat was my mother. Her breathing had become labored at some point after we had turned off the highway. It was nothing to immediately worry about, the doctors had assured us. 48 years of smoking could have that effect. Though she had stopped nearly twenty years ago, the damage was done. The black tar of that period adhering to her like layers of volcanic ash set deep within ancient stone.

I was her last living daughter, and she would not talk to

me. Not for a while, at least. Not in this state. Within moments, however, it was possible that she would think herself a child on the way to Ohio to visit relatives. Or perhaps she would turn and fail to recognize me. Were this to happen, she would likely have a panic attack and send us careening off the road into the accumulated bracken that seemed to stretch endlessly forward along the sides and in the ditches.

Ever since I had informed her we would be going up to the family cabin that had been constructed deep within the heart of the Cold Water Forest, the fact was never from from her mind. She had screamed and fanned her fists until the orderlies came to restrain her.

I still remember the look in their eyes. The weariness. The small spark of guilty joy that lay like the light at the end of a long tunnel. The knowledge that she would soon be leaving. Forever.

The blaze of her resistance had slowly ebbed and dissolved into a tough and rubbery obstinance. A refusal to talk or walk on her own. As if it was better to waste away to dust and bones than return to the old Norris cottage. Built by my grandfather after the second world war, it was a small, narrow building dug into the side of a hill. Instead of logs or brick, the cabin had been constructed out of sawn lumber.

I had gone there twice as a child and the image of it sticks hard in my memory. It was dank and cool, the small wood stove giving off insufficient heat for the cold fall that had settled in around us. I remember the brush and trees seeming to distance themselves from the structure, leaving a wide ring of beaten dirt around it as if it had just struck the ground like a meteor. I can't remember if this is something my mind had constructed but I also remember the peculiar fact that, despite a lack of maintenance, it never fell into disrepair but instead retained its creaky old image in perpetuity. As if it had had some long standoff with entropy and had drawn a stalemate.

Despite these oddities, I had never heard of anything bad happening there, so as far as I was concerned, my mother's strong dislike of the place was unfounded.

What her world must be. The slow brain disease gnawing away at her like a toothless mouth slowly gumming some small animal to death. Steadily. Arduously. Her experience of life a pile of mental photographs that gets kicked up by a gust of wind, only to flutter and fall all around her. Flashes of image and feeling.

For reasons I can't explain, I remember our arrival through Haylie's eyes. I think it's because, as a parent, you try to be aware of occurrences that might impress themselves on your child.

I'm sure the most unnerving thing was the sound. The shrieks. The utter transformation of my mother from a quiet fixture into a hissing, clawing, screaming, fighting demon. Dragging her from the car was difficult only because I wasn't expecting it to be a problem. In actuality, she only weighed about 90 pounds and once I had overcome the initial shock of her yelling inarticulately in my face, it was simply a matter of yanking her out.

Once she was out in the open air, however, it became a different story.

She began to claw at me. She wasn't strong but her nails were long and sharp. The first slash caught my cheek, the second one landing just below my left eye. A thin rivulet of blood running down my face, I staggered back and blinked away the tears that automatically sprang up.

My mother tried to run. I don't know where she thought she was going to go. Maybe back down the road, all the way to Minneapolis. Or maybe off into the woods like some wild thing that would scrabble through the brush until she collapsed from exhaustion, never to get back up again.

She wasn't fast, thankfully, and in a moment I had my arm wrapped around her waist and was dragging her backward toward the cabin.

How must we have looked to my daughter?

The headlights illuminating the two of us like a pair of fighting birds. Arms and curses being flung into the air as the night around us watched with silent solemnity. I dragged her kicking and screaming to the door where I had to hold her with a single arm as I fumbled with my keys.

The one I needed was about twice as large as all the others on my key chain, so finding it was easy enough. Turning it, however, was not. The ring of keys jangled as I struggled with the mechanism. Then I was twisting the knob, my mother slipping free and stumbling down the porch and tripping and collapsing into the dirt below.

A dry cloud of dust kicked up around her and hung suspended in the headlights. I looked at Haylie to make sure she was still there. She was. She was standing still, her arms wrapped around her chest, chin pointed down. Her body had the appearance of being skinny and formless, half-cloaked in shadow.

I thumped down the steps and swept up my mother and tossed her over my shoulder and the screaming erupted for a second time as I carried her rabid and unwilling out of the glare of the headlights and into the toothless mouth of the building.

2

The first night passed like a death watch. Haylie went to the small room at the back of the cabin and closed the door, blotting out the incessant moans. My mother did not sleep. Instead, she curled up and shrank into the corner opposite the wood stove, occasionally muttering to herself.

I sat there on an ancient futon wrapped in a blanked that smelled like the inside of the 1970s. The room was dark, the only light coming from a night light I had scrounged out of a junk drawer.

It had been a long day and I drifted in and out of sleep, the real world blurring into dream. The air was cool but heavy. It held yesterday's humidity like an anchor, refusing to let it float away.

At some point, I got up and put a quilt around my mother's shoulders. She was a dark blotch in the corner, the dim light illuminating only the edges of her body. If she wasn't going to lay down in a bed then so be it.

The nurses had said that she would often do this. They'd come in in the morning to find her scrunched up in the corner of the room, her knees pulled tightly to her chin.

Her moaning fell into a steady rhythm and eventually pulled me out of the shallow end of consciousness and into the numb expanse of sleep.

That night I dreamt that there was a troop of goblins marching steadily by the cabin's windows, their pointy ears passing like the tips of spears. They spoke in some foreign gurgle and rattled the doorknobs as they halted their progress and attempted to enter. Shining amphibious eyes rose in to peer through the windows, flickering in the feeble electric light of the interior.

At one point, my gaze locked with one of theirs. I didn't move. Couldn't if I wanted to. I could smell its noxious opioid breath drifting through the drafty walls that had been hammered into place by my grandfather.

A cold blue light eventually tinted the windows. I awoke with my eyes already open. Dry and burning. My mother had stopped moaning. The cabin was quiet. I got up to make sure she was still alive.

3

THAT MORNING, I BROUGHT IN A FEW BAGS OF GROCERIES I had left in the car overnight. It was mostly nonperishables like canned beans, canned tomatoes, and bags of rice. There was also a small box of powdered donuts for Haylie and some sliced bread and peanut butter.

That's what we had for breakfast.

There was a small table pushed up against the wall with some wooden chairs huddled around it, but it was so buried in magazines and ancient mail that I decided it would be best if we ate on the couch.

The peanut butter was thick and dry in my mouth and I had a hard time swallowing it. I would occasionally glance over the top of Haylie's head to see if my mother was having the same problem.

Her jaw worked mechanically, kneading the bread and peanut butter with her tongue and gums until it was wet enough to slide down her throat.

Haylie had no such problem with the donuts, unless you count eating six of them a problem. When she was done, she held her white, powdery hands out in front of her like a curious ghost, unsure of what to do with them. Eventually, she took to licking the dry sugar off of her fingertips and wiping them on her pants.

"Sleep alright, hun?"

She shrugged. "I miss my bed."

"This is our home now. A lot of things are going to seem new. It will take a while to get used to."

She was silent. The three of us sat there as the morning light drifted in through grimy window panes, the only sound being the light smacking of my mother's mouth as she worked dutifully to finish her breakfast.

"What's for lunch?" Haylie asked.

I sighed. "Honey, you just ate."

"So? We're still going to have lunch, right?"

"We'll have lunch. I haven't decided what to make."

She seemed to think about that for a moment.

"What are we going to do today?"

"I don't know. What do you want to do today?"

"What is there to do?"

I thought about the monumental task of cleaning the place but decided I wasn't going to win her over with that one.

"Wanna go for a walk? Check out the area?"

I saw her eyes bounce around the room, desperate for some way to entertain herself. She finally relented.

"I guess."

My mother eventually laid down in the other bedroom and drifted off almost immediately, her chest rising and falling steadily as I watched her. Finally certain she was asleep, I slipped out of the room and carefully let the door click closed behind me.

The property surrounding the cabin was massive. Rolling hills and dense brush were carved up and quartered by a network of winding trails. I knew there was a lake not far from here but I wasn't quite sure how to get to it.

Before we left, I rummaged through the junk drawer and eventually found an old compass. I leveled it in my hand, letting the needle settle. I turned until I was facing north and then once outside I did the same.

The sky overhead was oppressively overcast, obscuring the sun almost entirely. The trails I was looking for lay somewhere to the Southeast. To the West was the road we had come in on and to the North stretched a massive swamp.

Placing the compass in my pocket, I waited for Haylie, who emerged about a minute later wearing an old maroon windbreaker that had once been her brother's. The sleeves were too long for her short arms and she left it unzipped, letting it billow out behind her as she pounded down the steps.

The sight of the windbreaker was like a steel blade pushing into my stomach. I turned away toward the trail as I got myself under control.

We worked our way south, the path before us winding in and out of the forest. This part of the region had seen little-to-no logging or forest maintenance, so a great heap of blown down trees had accumulated on the forest floor. The gnarled roots and branches coalesced to create something akin to a jumble of limbs pointing in every direction, as if the forest had been thrown into a large bag, shaken up, and then dumped back out again.

I found my eyes searching the dark crevices for movement. Here and there some small mammals would scurry in and out of the dense brush, thin tails flicking. It was only after about the fourth one that I noticed something strange. It must have been in the movement or the way it held itself. Or maybe it was the way they seemed to slink around. What probably gave it away though was seeing—really seeing—one of the tails.

They weren't squirrels. They were rats.

I instinctively grabbed Haylie's head and turned it toward me, feeling a shiver run down my back. The forest felt suddenly dead. As if we had turned up to see something beautiful, only to find the corpse of what we had been expecting.

There was another rustle of dead branches and I felt Haylie's head turn in my hand, trying to get a look.

"Mom, why are there so many?" She must have seen.

"This is just a bad part of the woods," I said, picking up my pace. "C'mon. The lake should be close. I can see a clearing up ahead."

I hoped it was a clearing. The trees were sparse in this part and it was difficult to tell what lie ahead by looking at the tops of them. Still, it appeared the forest ended abruptly just a couple hundred feet down the trail. All we needed to do now was crest the tiny ridge of the hill that lay in front of us.

We hurried on and as we did I noticed something that I hadn't before. Except for an occasional chitter here and there, there was very little birdsong. I thought back, trying to remember if that was normal for this part, but I couldn't think back that far.

That oddity was swiftly knocked out of my mind however when the lake finally came into view.

Stretching out past the boundaries of sight, it lay there like something alien to our world, slowly suffocating beneath our atmosphere. Tepid foam lapped a soggy shoreline giving off an air of toxicity and decay. The lake that I had remembered was almost totally gone. The swamp immediately next to it had swarmed in along the banks, sending legions of tall weeds almost out into the middle. Here and there a dead tree stood frozen against the sky like the imprint of human ash against stone after some great ecological disaster.

If I had not seen it as a girl, I truly could not have called it a lake.

I turned to look at Haylie. She seemed unfazed by its appearance, seemingly more in tune with this place than I was.

"Can I go swimming?" She asked.

I was disturbed by the question but I tried not to let it show on my face. Maybe she wasn't so in tune with the place after all.

"I don't think so. The mud is deep in some parts." It was the best I could think of on the fly but it sounded feasible enough. "Maybe we'll do some fishing on the shoreline sometime."

I didn't actually want to eat anything that came out of that lake but we'd eventually have to find another way to bring in food. We couldn't live on rice and beans forever. Or at least, I couldn't.

"What's its name?"

"What?"

"What's its name?" Haylie repeated. "The lake."

"I don't know," I answered truthfully.

Thinking back, the lake had never had a name. We just called it "the lake."

Was it possible, I wondered to myself. Possible for a thing to lay here for so long in this world and never attract a name?

We plodded around the lake for a bit, trying to see if we could discern any more trails. We stumbled across a few that seemed to snake off into the encroaching marshland but none that promised better scenery than we were already getting, which wasn't much.

Haylie slapped her arm for about the hundredth time since we had arrived and pulled her hand away to reveal a splotch of blood just above her wrist.

"That must have been on you for a while," I said. "Better the bloodsuckers that fly than the ones that swim though. I bet the leeches around here could drain a dog in about four minutes."

I immediately regretted the comment. Convincing Haylie that being up here was the best move for us at the moment had been a nearly insurmountable task, one that eventually defaulted to me having to play the "because I said so" card. Surely her experiences thus far hadn't endeared her to my family's old property but she seemed marvelously unperturbed by all of it, as if she had accepted her fate and was now assessing the situation coldly like a scientist appraising some new discovery.

We eventually found a trail that looked like it headed off in the right direction and we began to follow it. It took us in and out of a large copse of trees and then sent us meandering back toward the cabin.

As we walked, I heard the scratch of bark and we both turned around. The wind was light and the tops of the trees swayed ever so slightly. There was nothing. As I was turning back, however, I caught sight of Haylie's face and stopped cold.

Her eyes were wide, her complexion pale. She was

looking in the same direction I had just been. Up toward the tops of the trees. I slowly turned to follow her gaze.

They were empty.

I turned back to her. "What is it?"

She didn't answer. Her gaze remained fixed at some singular point behind us. Then she slowly began to turn her head back to the trail, her eyes eventually following.

I refused to let it go. "Haylie," I said with a little more urgency. "What is it? Did you see something?"

She seemed to take a moment to consider the question.

"No," she finally said. Then, as if to undercut her own answer, she turned and looked back again. She let her gaze linger for a few solid seconds and I couldn't help but follow her line of sight again. Still nothing.

The rest of the walk back, I felt as if the stars above had just opened their eyes for the first time in centuries, watching our slow progress through the rat-infested landscape.

4

WE ATE A SMALL LUNCH OF BLACK BEANS ON CORN TORTILLAS. It felt good to get some more food into my belly but I could already tell that this kind of meal would get old fast. This meant that I either had to find the fishing poles that were buried somewhere in the cabin's basement or make the long drive back into town to get some groceries.

Aside from certain financial barriers, I loathed the idea of having to shove my mother back into a car and relive the scene from the previous night.

She seemed to have settled in reasonably well. After having lunch with us, she shuffled back to her room to read. There were several dusty large print mysteries stacked up in the bedroom closet and while I doubted she'd be able to follow the plots very well, she seemed to be more motivated by reflex than anything else, as if the act of reading was the goal in itself, the story secondary.

Haylie, on the other hand, had reached her threshold of boredom so quickly that it ended up pushing her into the basement to look for something to do. She ended up reemerging about twenty minutes later with a sketchpad and an ancient box of crayons just as I was finishing up washing the dishes.

As someone who had been accustomed to a dishwasher in our previous apartment, the work felt laborious and unnecessary. And while my rational mind knew it was something I had taken for granted all those years, it still grated on my nerves. Thankfully, with few people and little food, the task was done quickly enough.

"Mom, I'm going to go draw outside."

"Ok," I replied, then added, "Stay close."

That insidious feeling of being watched began to creep up the base of my neck again and I tried to shake it off.

After the door slapped shut behind her, I plopped down on the couch, let my head tilt back, and closed my eyes for a moment.

The amount of sleep I had gotten the night before was negligible, plus I was never a heavy sleeper to begin with. Even as a child, I would frequently wake up and lay in bed thinking. Then as I got older and the problems began to stack up, it seemed my body's capacity for rest had been diminished, replaced by the urgency of the modern world.

My head snapped forward and I rubbed my eyes. I had fallen asleep. Turning to look at the clock, I nearly had a heart attack when I realized my mother was sitting on the couch next to me, her cloudy blue eyes prodding me.

Her skin was sallow, her eyes sunken. The long stringy hair that fell past her shoulders was a mixture of grey and white. Her shrewd, pincer-like lips were pursed and turned down in a perpetual frown.

"I can't leave," she said. Her voice was quiet. Weak.

"No," I agreed. There wasn't much more I could say on the matter. She was right. She couldn't leave. Not unless she wanted to go hiking back into town.

Then she said something I didn't understand.

"I'm here. I've always been here."

"Excuse me?"

"I..." Her face twisted. "I can feel my soul...leaking out of me. It's here in this place. Like cement around my feet."

I didn't answer. She got like this sometimes. I decided to ride it out silently.

"It's leaking into me too. Like a dripping faucet. I can feel it around my neck...I-" She lifted a bony hand to her throat and pulled the top of her shirt down as she began to rub it.

Before she could do anything, I reached over and tugged her shirt down even further to make sure I had seen what I thought I had. Something like electricity surged through me as I observed the heavy bruise and ligature marks that wrapped their way around her neck.

"Mom, where did you get this bruise?" I asked urgently.

She didn't answer. Instead, she just continued rubbing. I repeated the question but she remained silent.

Then an unnerving thought struck me. Had I done this? Last night as I dragged her into the cabin? I thought for sure I had had my arms around her waist but...

No. That couldn't be. It had to be something else. Someone else. At the nursing home, probably. That had to be it.

Relief began to dull the edges of the fear that had been clenching my gut. In taking her out of the home, I must have unwittingly taken her from the grasp of someone—some abuser. That figured. Those people. People called them "caretakers" but I knew better. There was no such thing as a caretaker. Or a helper. It was all vanity. A money-making scheme. Doctors. Nurses. The whole lot of them. Totally worthless.

"You're safe now," I said. "I don't know who did this to

you but they can't hurt you here. They probably don't even know where you are. This address shouldn't be in anyone's files."

She didn't respond. Instead, she just kept twisting her face and flexing her jaw.

I spent the next couple minutes returning her to bed and letting her know she was safe. After getting her under the covers and trying to soothe her, I left and gently shut the door behind me.

I let out a breath. For the first time since I had arrived, I had the strong urge to have a drink. Unfortunately, we hadn't quite had enough money for that sort of thing when we had gone to the store and I didn't typically drink enough for the matter to warrant any second thought.

Now that I was here though, I was regretting that decision. I had quit smoking almost a year ago and—other than chewing my fingernails—hadn't found a suitable distraction, and I could sure as hell use one now.

Fishing poles. Yeah, maybe I'd go try and scrounge those up. Unfortunately, that meant going down into the dark and cluttered basement.

5

———

I HAVE BEEN IN A LOT OF CABINS IN MY LIFE, ESPECIALLY BACK when I was dating Luis, my future husband. Luis came from a pretty well-to-do family who inexplicably didn't seem to like me very much. They tolerated me, however, at least enough to allow me into their summer cottage. Well, they called it a "cottage" but in actuality, it was a five-bedroom lake house nicer than any house I had lived in growing up. Luis and I spent a lot of time there in our years together and it would eventually be the place where he voided his insurance policy all over the walls.

Back when we were dating, we would occasionally head up to one of his friends' cabins, which might as well have been the same as the one owned by my in-laws. Jacuzzis. Indoor pools. Speed boats. Outdoor saunas. These were practically the building blocks for what these people called "cabins."

The Norris cabin on the other hand, had a hand-pump well out back, a two-hole outhouse, and an absolute carcass of a lake that was about a mile away. To put it bluntly: the

Norris cabin was a shit hole and the basement was arguably the worst part of it.

Ancient mail heaped in piles. Boxes of junk to which no single thing could be given a name or purpose. And to top it all off; it was dark and dusty and the walls looked like they were bending inward, giving it a sort of haunted carnival fun-house aesthetic.

I began to dig.

I knew we had fishing poles somewhere. I distinctly remembered my mom and dad using them one summer at the edge of the lake while my sister and I played in the weeds. We had stalked through the tall vegetation in our bare feet as we hunted leopard frogs, their slim camouflaged bodies zipping away from us like underwater arrows.

My sister Alina had died of a drug overdose eight years later, and now it seemed that the last refuge for those good memories had begun to die as well, as if the needle she had put in her arm that day had pierced her paper-thin skin and gone directly into the very core of her essence, killing everything it was attached to.

I remember when I was a teenager, my mom came home one day to find me holding a dead blackbird that had crashed into our window. It was still warm. She told me that this was an important moment. That the bird had hatched from an egg some time ago and been reared by its own mother, fed and encouraged to fly. Maybe even had its own babies. Its own daughter. It had lived an intricate life and in that life, there had been a billion meaningful occurrences until one day it had endured its final one.

She then told me that every single life had a million lives in it and that the world was not a straight line. She said that it was an unknowable number of wayward threads colliding infinitely with each other. And that blackbird had just collided with us—with the thread of our family and our home—and been destroyed. She then explained to me that one day we would endure the same thing. The end of our thread. Our fate. We would collide with an impassable barrier and all of the things we were connected to would shift like the ground beneath our feet. The very notion of what the world was would change.

That's what I felt now, thinking about Alina's death. It was as if she had been attached to this place in a way and her passing had cut the lifelines to some crucial aspects of the environment. Sure, it had always felt rustic and disorganized but there was something missing that had been here before. Something different. Or at least that's how it felt to me.

It was also possible that it had always been like this. Perhaps the wonder goggles of childhood had allowed me to perceive it as some magical land, when it was just this all along. Full of rats and bad dreams.

The whole thing made me wonder what other aspects of the world I had perceived incorrectly. What aspect of it was I misunderstanding at this very moment.

It went on and on like that in my head as I rummaged through the junk. The task seemed almost impossible. I would pick something up to try and organize it but there was nowhere to put it. The place was a traffic jam of garbage, where nothing could be moved without moving the entirety of it.

I thought about that. Thought about what it would take to just jettison the entire contents of the cellar into some nearby landfill or gulley. A lot of effort, surely, but it was hard to imagine it would require more than cleaning it.

Just then, I moved a tilted box aside to reveal an ancient black rotary phone sitting atop a small wooden stool. The phone appeared to be hooked up to the wall so I picked up the receiver and listened to the dial tone. There wasn't one.

What there was however made my throat involuntarily clench shut.

On the other end of the line, traveling across who knew how many miles of wire, there was the steady sound of someone breathing.

"Hello?" I said tentatively. It came out choked.

Nothing.

I repeated myself, this time a little more confident. "Hello."

Still nothing.

I slammed the receiver down and took a breath. Of course, it wasn't someone breathing. Chances were the phone line wasn't even hooked up to anything. It probably just ran outside somewhere and the wire was scraping against something in the wind. Or one of those damn rats was chewing on it somewhere, hopefully not inside the cabin.

After placing the box back in its place, I tilted my head back and sighed. The ceiling above me was open, wires and pipes running over my head like a network of disparate highways. I glanced around the room. A few rays of light in adjacent windows crisscrossed over half of the floor, illuminating whirls of dust that I had kicked up in my search.

It seemed suddenly unlikely to me that fishing poles would be lying under a bunch of boxes, so instead of aimlessly shifting junk around, I began looking in places I might keep them. First, I checked all four corners, then did my best to make my way along the edge of the wall where it met the floor, thinking someone may have laid them flat there.

That's when I came across the second odd discovery of the afternoon.

If it weren't for the lock on the outside I wouldn't have seen it. Near the corner opposite the bottom of the stairs leaned a large piece of plywood and just to the right of that was the dull knob of a swing latch lock. Curious, I pushed the piece of plywood away to reveal a small 4x4 foot door cut into the wall.

My mind began to do the calculation.

The wall wasn't thick so the door must have led outside rather than into some space within the cabin. But wait—I took a moment to orient myself—if my thinking was correct then this was on the hill-side of the building, so the door probably went into the hill.

Why? Why would they need to make a door down here, especially one that, in all likelihood, didn't go anywhere?

Probably full of fucking fishing poles.

I tried the latch. At first, I didn't think it was going to move. It seemed pretty stuck in place and due to my unfamiliarity with the kind of lock, I wasn't even sure I was doing it correctly. Then, as I pushed up, there was a metallic clank as it finally released.

When I tried to open the door itself, however, I soon found that it was so tightly wedged into place that it probably didn't even need a lock. Decades of brutally cold winters, humid summers, and shifting earth had warped the wood around the frame so much that I'd probably have had an easier time kicking a hole in the wall.

You would have thought that the rest of the house would have been similarly warped, but for reasons I couldn't explain, the basement walls seemed to be the only part that had succumbed to the ravages of the seasons.

After a solid minute of pulling, I relented and gave up. It

was stuck. I had a tire iron in my car that I might have been able to use to wedge it open but my feeling was that it was too wide to get under the barely visible crack at the bottom where the door met the floor. Maybe a large flathead screwdriver?

Maybe later. The last thing I wanted to do was pry off a piece of the cabin's wall from the inside and let some godawful hill creatures inside. There were already rats in the woods, so I was happy not to give them a nice new access way into the place where I currently slept.

Still feeling a little uneasy about the door's existence, I replaced the plywood and pushed a few heavy boxes up against it. From inside one of the boxes came the rattle of something faintly recognizable, like trinkets in a tin can. I opened it up and sure enough, my grandfather's old tackle box. And alongside it?

A pair of old cream-colored fishing poles from the 80s. They were both broken down and had the reels removed but some further digging brought out a few extra reels as well, and about thirty minutes later I had them both assembled and ready to go. The fishing line left something to be desired and I didn't have a lot of confidence in it if I hooked into something big but hopefully, it would be enough for a few perch or small bass.

I closed up the box, gathered the fishing supplies, and hauled it all upstairs. I wouldn't think about the door again until about two days later when my eyes shot open in the middle of the night.

6

———

THE NEXT DAY, WE WENT BACK TO THE LAKE TO TRY OUR HAND at some fishing. I woke up early in the morning, just a few minutes before sunrise. The cool air hit me as I stepped outside, morning fog instantly clinging to my skin. Clean bucket in hand, I made my way to the well, hung it on the hand crank for a moment, and then made my way to the outhouse. Once inside, I sat down on the cold plastic toilet seat that had been placed over one of the two wooden holes where we did our business.

The room was dank and lit by nothing but a small murky window cut into the side. During the night, I would have brought a lantern or flashlight out but I figured it was light enough now, which turned out to be somewhat incorrect. I managed though, and when I was finished, I used an old coffee can to scoop a handful of lye out of one of the heavy paper bags we kept in the corner and tossed the chalky substance down the hole.

There have certainly been more desirable morning restroom experiences, but in the grand history of the world, there have also been worse.

Once I had stepped back out into the morning air, I walked over to the hand pump that was fed from our underground well and began to crank water into a bucket. When it was about 3/4 full, I lugged it back inside and set it on the countertop. I then fished a few mugs out of the cabinet, ladled some water into them, and set them down next to the bucket.

Haylie's door opened just as I was finishing up and she stepped out into the living area rubbing her eyes.

"Get dressed, honey, we're gonna go fishing."

"Right now? It's so early."

"It's when the fish are hungry."

"That's dumb. I'm hungry all day," she said. Then she turned around and walked back into her bedroom.

After a few seconds of waiting, I began to suspect that she had just laid back down instead of getting dressed, and when I walked into her room my theory was confirmed. We did our back and forth for a few more minutes and then we were finally headed down toward the lake.

The rats were still there, of course, the sounds of their sharp little feet scratching over the wood, but as we walked it slowly became easier to just pretend they were squirrels. In a way, they were squirrels. They just happened to not have any hair on their tails.

I tried to keep telling myself that until we had finally reached the shoreline.

Fishing was something of a misadventure, but not wholly so. The old line broke half-a-dozen times and we had to use whatever bugs or worms we could find under rocks and dead trees. The stench of decay was on the air again as it had been yesterday, the odor of soggy dead things bumping up against the sandy beach.

"What's that smell?" Haylie asked, scrunching up her

nose. She waved the end of her fishing pole around in the air like a dead sparkler.

"It's the swamp," I said. "And the water."

"Why does it smell so bad though?"

"Most of the water back ho-" I stopped and corrected myself. "-back in our old apartment was run through a filter."

"What about the water out back? Is that run through a filter?"

I tried to think about the construction of the well out back and whether or not it had a filter, but couldn't for the life of me remember. That is, if I had ever known in the first place.

"I don't think so," I said. "But that water is held in the ground way, way down where living things can't get at it."

"So," Haylie worked through that in her mind for a second, "is the smell dead things then?"

"Yes," I answered reluctantly. "And living things. A lot of things live and die around water. And when they do it's...smelly."

That seemed to pacify her for the moment. A breeze lifted both of our fishing lines in the air and then set them back down again, the light ripples marching steadily away over the surface of the water.

"Did Jacob die in water?"

Something clenched inside of my chest and I felt a familiar ache travel up through my throat. I wrestled it down as I always did, wondering absentmindedly if tears would show themselves this time. They didn't.

"No," I answered after a while. "I told you, he died in the hospital."

"Does that mean he didn't smell?"

"Don't talk about your brother like that."

She was quiet for a long time after that. We stood there silently in the cool fall day, the smell of rot permeating our skin. When I finally pulled a small perch in, I looked over to see if Haylie was excited but her eyes stared straight ahead, out over the water.

I was dreaming. I was in a city, though I couldn't tell which one. The lights were dull and muted, as if they were straining against an oppressive darkness. An empty, rain-sodden street stretched out before me and something cold and jelly-like rested in the pit of my legs, telling me I wouldn't be able to run very fast if I tried. The moon was nowhere to be seen. No trace of stars or clouds. The sky was a black smudge, so much so that I could have been convinced I was underground.

I turned and saw that half a block away was a phone booth with a red telephone inside. It wasn't ringing but it pulled me toward it, nonetheless. Possessing the magnetism and finality of dream logic, I was drawn forward. My heels clacked in the empty streets. I pulled my black wool coat tighter around me.

When I got to the booth, I discovered that the cloudy glass door was held shut by the swing latch lock that had secured the small door downstairs. I pulled it up but it wouldn't open. Leaning all of my weight into it, I placed the palm of my hand against the furthermost side of the latch and forced it straight up with a crooked arm.

Without warning, the door blasted open and I was washed in fetid air. Some sort of mammalian musk and rotting fish. It now seemed as if I couldn't step into that booth if I had been dragged in on a leash. The tightly enclosed area ignited some primal warning in the base of my brain, overriding any kind of logic that might persuade me to enter.

But then the next second I was standing in it, the door shut, the phone in my hand. I placed the receiver to my ear.

Over the line came a rapid snuffling. I slammed the receiver back down and spun to leave.

As I did however, I caught a glimpse of something approaching from down the street.

It couldn't be mistaken for anything else. Maybe in real life it could. But not here. Not in this dream where everything was simultaneously known to me and irrevocably warped beyond comprehension.

It was a rat. Massive and hulking, it dragged its swollen belly over the pockmarked asphalt on legs that could barely support it. Its face was sunken and punctuated with pale sightless eyes. At the end of its long curving snout was the writhing inflamed flesh of its feverishly searching nostrils.

I stumbled headfirst out of the booth, breaking a heel on the curb. Pain flared up my leg and my knees felt as if they were on two perfectly rotating ball bearings, unable to stay upright for any length of time. I gasped and tried to cry for help but there was no sound. Nothing but the greedy sniffing that echoed in my ears.

My legs finally failing, I began to drag myself down the street. I reached my hand out and noticed that my wedding ring was gone, the slender digit appearing suddenly naked without it. No stone. No eternal golden band. Just me, breaking my nails against the pavement as I tried to claw myself to safety.

Something cold and wet touched my bare calf and I sobbed. I was now stuck there, trapped in a web of IV tubes that had appeared so suddenly it was as if they had been there the whole time. I rolled and twisted, trying to get free.

The light above was suddenly blinding. Cold fluorescent lights and sterile walls. Hot rodent breath pouring over my face in a mixture of sweet vomit, disinfectant, and rotting flesh.

I cried out, but there was no one. I cried for my mother but she wasn't there. No one was there. I was alone in a cold room while the rat stared down at me, its eyes a pair of dead fluorescent lights that buzzed like flies. It used its scrabbling little fingers that bent and twisted in every direction to scratch and claw at my belly, pulling the ropes of my intestines out, the thick guts slapping against the grimy tile below.

Then the rat gathered them all up in its arms like a bundle of yarn and turned and unlocked the door that was the hidden cellar door and darted out into the night but the intestines were still attached and it pulled tight and snapped me forward, dragging me through the door as I kicked and screamed and begged but there was no one and nothing and the black night air bent down and licked the side of my face.

My eyes shot open and I lurched up off the futon, almost falling to the floor. I caught myself and slowly stood, my hands shaking. I peered around the room, my vision not yet able to make out the darkened forms. As it adjusted, my heart rate began to slow down to a normal rhythm.

I was at the cabin. My mother and daughter sleeping in their respective rooms not ten feet away. It was a dream. A nightmare. Nothing else. But then I noticed something that made my blood run cold.

I lifted my hand and touched the side of my face. It was wet.

It wasn't the slick sheen of sweat that comes in the night but the slime of saliva. I furiously wiped my face and peered around again, looking harder this time. I padded softly through the cramped room, looking behind furniture and under the futon. I walked over and checked the lock on the door and then back to make sure Haylie and my mother were still sleeping.

They were, each of them breathing softly in the steady rhythm of sleep. That left one other place.

The basement door opened to a hard right that sent you down a steep flight of bare wooden steps. In all of my grandfather's infinite wisdom, he had neglected to place a light on the upper level which gave anyone who wanted to go down the steps in the night a short but nerve-wracking journey to the bottom. Once down there, they would then have to swing their arms invisibly out in front of them until they came across the dangling string of the single lightbulb that served to illuminate the cluttered disaster of the Norris cabin's basement.

Feeling my heart begin to race again, I quickly went through the process until the bulb sprang to life overhead in a dim amber glow, casting the mountains of junk in a feverish orange hue, making it look like the underworld's mailroom.

The heavy boxes were where I had left them, the door still locked and blockaded. I breathed a sigh of relief and returned up the steps. As I plodded back upstairs the darkness settled back in around me, along with the brisk chill of abandonment.

7
____

Haylie and I spent the afternoons fishing. Something about the specific geographical region seemed to funnel as many clouds our way as possible and I began to feel as if I hadn't seen the sun for days. Days stretched into weeks as dried leaves began to fall and collect on the ground. Our food supplies grew thin until there was nothing left but what we pulled from the lake and a few sacred cans of baked beans I was keeping for a special occasion.

My mother didn't complain, which was honestly surprising to me. All she seemed to do now was sleep or sit on her bed and read. Occasionally I would wake to find her in the corner or come into her room in the morning to find her huddled in a ball of blankets on the floor. But for the most part, she seemed stable. Predictable.

A sort of routine settled in. We'd fish in the morning then head back and eat around 10:00am. For the rest of the day, I'd continue the project of cleaning out the basement while Haylie went outside to play. We lost track of the days. The months.

Cold winds began blowing through the hills as the sun

set earlier and earlier. We soon found ourselves firing up the wood stove nearly every night. It got me thinking about winter and I soon shifted my focus from the basement to gathering up firewood.

There was a rusty wood ax hanging up on the wall of the outhouse but whenever I tried to split wood with it, the blade would either get stuck in the log or hit at an odd angle and send it careening off in any direction. Eventually, I gave up and just started gathering pieces of wood that were about as thick as my forearm. Lord knew there was enough of it lying around. All I had to do was go lopping pieces off and force all of my concentration away from whatever skittered over my foot.

All in all, life was tough but manageable. That is, until the day we received a visitor. A stranger carrying both the past and—though I didn't know it at the time—a litany of ill omens.

He came just after 2:00PM. I was inside washing a heavy layer of tree sap from my hands. A large pine branch had fallen just in front of the cabin steps the night before and I had had to drag it to the edge of the woods with my bare hands, leaving half of it lying within the circle of tan grass that surrounded the cabin and the other half conjoined to the endless sea of downed bracken.

Just as I was finishing wiping my hands on a dishrag, there was a crisp knock on the door. At first, I thought I had imagined it. I waited for a second, letting the reality of the sound sink in. Then I rushed to the door simultaneously believing that it was Haylie who had gotten locked out somehow and a debt collector with a baseball bat and a sock full of quarters.

It was neither.

When I opened the door, relief flooded through me as I recognized the snappy blue postman uniform. The man looked to be in his early thirties with thinning chestnut hair less than half an inch in length and a tall and wiry figure that would have made him ideal for reaching the expensive boxes of cereal in grocery stores. He was lanky, a little boyish, and immediately disarming.

"How may I help you?" I asked, a decade's worth of retail training overriding any other logical thing one might say to a stranger.

"Are you Kelsey Fletcher?" the man asked, his eyebrows rising so far up they almost erased his forehead.

I hesitated. I was, of course, but how did he know that. Well, from the mail obviously, but how had mail found its way to me here? And more importantly, why did this man see fit to drive all the way in here instead of placing the mail in the box at the end of the drive?

"Your box is pretty full," he said, which was one question answered. "Plus, I wanted to make sure it wasn't a mistake. It's been so long and, well—I guess I wanted to see if there was someone really living out here or not."

"Thanks," I said hesitantly. I reached out and grabbed the stack of envelopes from his hand. "I shouldn't be getting mail though. No one knows I'm up here."

"Someone does," the mailman said. He shifted on his feet, looking like he wanted to say more.

I looked him over. He seemed energetic. A little skittish.

"Who knows I'm up here-" I squinted at his tiny name badge, "-Preston?"

The man's gaze slid to the floor and then back up again. "So you gotta understand: I didn't go through your mail or nothing. I just-"

"What?"

"We thought it might be the wrong address is all. We didn't look inside the envelope but we saw that one of those letters was from a debt collection agency and we figured—" He shrugged his shoulders. "Well, they're pretty good at finding people."

"So you saw that it was from a collection agency and figured I must be staying up here, that it?"

"Pretty much," he said, nodding. "Hey look, this isn't even my route. I volunteered for this delivery. Most of the guys don't want to come up here for any reason, even if they're curious."

I closed my eyes, trying to prioritize all of my questions. I started with the most obvious one.

"Why don't people want to come up here?" I asked.

The man tilted his head back and forth. "Ya know, this place kinda has a reputation. These parts I mean. The area."

"Oh yeah?"

"Well, yeah. Of course." He looked confused. "Surely you gotta know that."

His eyebrows knit together and he looked down at one of the envelopes.

"You are Kelsey Fletcher, right? I asked that?"

"Yup," I drew the word out, trying to think. "What kind of reputation?" Then, because he didn't seem the type to be transparent without an infuriating amount of prodding, "If you don't mind. Please. I've only been here a few times when I was a kid. Seemed fine to me though."

"Does it seem fine to you now?"

I should have seen it coming but the comment caught me off guard. Of course it didn't. For all of my little denials and making the best of the situation, the place didn't seem all right. Not one bit, now that I was thinking about it.

"Haven't you ever heard the story about the two girls who lost a horse while riding on the trails? It's an old one but surely you must have heard. Or what about the disappearances? Or the time the park ranger stumbled into your family's swamp?"

"No, none of it," I was shaking my head, bewildered. "What happened to the park ranger?"

"Yeah, sure," Preston seemed eager to tell the story. A little too eager in my opinion. I had put his age at about 30 when I first saw him but now I wasn't so sure. Maybe he was just a little...young for his age. I had certainly known a few small-town folks who ended up that way. A few city people too now that I was thinking about it.

"It was about 15 years ago now," he explained. "Ranger stumbles into your swamp and loses all connection. Went missing for six days. Then when they found him he just... wasn't right, ya know?"

I shook my head. "Not really. No."

"Yeah sure," Preston said again and I realized the phrase must have been somewhat compulsive for him. "He goes home. Won't talk. Won't eat. Two weeks later the guy kills his whole family. Everything in the house. Wife, kids, dog. They found him in the basement hunting down the fucking daddy long legs with a bottle of spray paint."

He looked suddenly abashed.

"Pardon the language, ma'am."

"That's ok, I don't think 'fuck' was the worst thing you said in the last ten seconds."

How did I not know about this? The place was dreary, sure, but dead families? Jesus.

Then again, I'd never done any digging into the town or the property. Never looked up the news or anything. And by the time I had the idea to come up here, my mom was already declining in health.

"So that begs the question," I said. "Why are you out here?"

At this, the guy's cheeks flushed red. He shrugged, another compulsion.

"I don't know," he said. "I just kinda like...spooky stuff, ya know? UFOs. Bigfoot. That's kinda my thing."

"You believe in Bigfoot?" I asked.

"Of course, you don't?"

"Not particularly."

"Let me ask you a question then: why not?" He said the words as if they were the ultimate 'gotcha' statement.

"I don't know," I said, shaking my head. "I guess I think we probably would have seen him by now. And don't give me any bullshit about government suppressing facts. A bunch of suits couldn't care less about some ape-man running around in the woods and throwing his poop at tourists."

Preston laughed. "No, no. No government suppression. It's simply a matter of mythologizing."

"Mythologizing?"

"Yeah, sure. There's a sort of veil, you see. It happened at the time of enlightenment. We traded something for something else."

"What do you mean?" I asked.

"I mean we relegated things into two categories: fact and myth. And we don't allow them to touch. And if some truth doesn't become a fact in a certain amount of time, then it becomes a myth. And once it's a myth it can't go back."

"I'm not sure I'm following."

"What I'm saying is, the idea of Bigfoot and aliens and all of that have spent so much time in the realm of myth that even if we were to be handed incontrovertible evidence of one's existence, it would remain a myth. Part of it is because we're simply too stubborn and afraid to believe in outrageous things. As a society, I mean. But another part is that when something becomes a fact it suffers a sort of degradation."

"I'm not sure I agree," I said hesitantly. "A fact is a fact. It's reality. A myth is just a lie."

"Don't be so sure," Preston said. He raised his index finger, a beaming smile on his face.

I leaned against the door frame, beginning to regret engaging him in the first place.

"Our ancestors didn't have a way of recording history in the way we do so they spent millions of years developing a sophisticated way of codifying knowledge. Our brains are prone to myth and narrative. We understand it better than facts and statistics. In some ways, this hurts us, leaving us open to any kind of interpretation of the world or unfolding events. But in another way, there are things we understand symbolically that we can't articulate. Mythology isn't a lie so much as it is a form of dream. An understanding of something bigger than the words we might use to try and capture them."

"Are you saying that Bigfoot is a...dream?"

"No." The mailman smiled. "What I'm saying is, there are these two worlds and we don't let them touch. The problem is, in reality, they do touch."

"Preston," I held out my hand and smiled. "Nice meeting you. Thanks for the mail. Please leave it in the box next time."

"Sorry," he laughed. "This place just gets me going, ya know? As I said, it's kind of my thing. Anyway, you've got a bunch of old mail in your box and you'll have to clean it out before I can use it."

"Can't you just like, throw it in the weeds or something?"

"Sorry, ma'am. That would be a federal crime."

I agreed to go clean out the mailbox when I got the time and he said goodbye before his little grey hatchback with the yellow light on top made a tight turn and exited down our drive. Once he was gone, I breathed a sigh of relief.

The guy was weird, to be sure, but when I had heard the knock I had thought the worst. Daydreams of dower-looking men wearing sunglasses and hefting baseball bats filled my mind. I knew that wasn't the way debt collectors operated these days but the images in my head felt much closer to the truth.

Haylie came inside soon after and asked if there was any mail for her. I was somewhat loath to actually look through it so I had left it in a heap on the counter. I gestured at it dismissively and she began to sort through it, looking for anything with her name on it.

"Nothing," she said, dejected.

"Nothing is right." I walked over and sat down on the couch. "I'm going to get dinner going in a few moments here. Can you go out back and pump some water while I heat things up?"

"That doesn't look like getting dinner ready," she said flatly.

"I said in a *few moments*. Can you please just go do what I asked?"

Haylie rolled her eyes and started banging through the cupboards.

"We're out of clean cups," she said.

"Did you wash them this morning?"

"Did *you* wash them this morning?"

It went on like that, the evening shot through with tension. I'm not sure if it was being reminded of the outside world by the mailman or just a young girl slowly succumbing to boredom, but she was particularly troublesome until she went to bed.

10

———

THAT NIGHT I HAD ANOTHER NIGHTMARE.

I was walking through a forest of white trees, their red leaves slowly falling one by one to the ground. I heard a commotion up ahead and rushed forward to find my husband, Luis, chasing blackbirds around a small glade with a double-barrel shotgun broken open in his right arm. Every once in a while he would catch one of the birds and proceed to shove it into one of the open chambers.

I stood there watching as he gradually captured each and every bird. Then without warning, he made eye contact with me across the glade, placed the barrel of the shotgun in his mouth, and pulled the trigger.

My scream was drowned out by an explosion of black wings as the birds rocketed into the branches behind him, knocking all of their red leaves to the ground at once.

I awoke, my eyes burning. I reached up to wipe them. As I did, however, I noticed that something was wrong.

For one, I was standing upright. I blinked a few times and tried to let my eyes adjust. But I already knew where I was. It was hard not to. The hard thing was believing it.

The thing that hit me first was the smell. Never in my life had something smelled so much like life and death simultaneously. All around me was a cacophony of croaking frogs and chiming insects. My feet were sunk into the boggy bottom of some shallow pool of water. Dead, lanky trees reached in silent praise against the backdrop of a despondently blue nighttime sky.

I was in the swamp. Panic growing in my chest, I began to walk.

There was no sign of the cabin. No flickering light or break in the trees ahead. There was just the raw and ancient wilderness, existing as it always had. As it always would. Human civilization nothing but a passing rumor from far-off lands. I kept stopping to shake my head, hoping I would wake up. But I didn't.

As I splashed forward, I felt my lips begin to quiver. I pushed the feeling down, replacing it with what I knew. I was in the swamp. It was night. Where and at what time I didn't know. I took a brief moment to be thankful for the unseasonably weather. On a different night I could have easily died of hypothermia.

Still time for that, something inside of me whispered. I picked up my pace and then stopped.

What if I was heading in the wrong direction? I closed my eyes and tried to think. What surrounded the swamp? Forest, I was pretty sure. But wasn't there a road that wrapped its way around it? Yeah, but how far?

My thoughts were cut off by a splash to my left. I froze, turning my head. I couldn't make anything out. In the wilted moonlight, everything was amorphously threatening. Every shape and pool of darkness a possible threat.

Another splash. This one closer and more of a swish through the water. Whatever it was, it was bigger than a rat. And if it was a rat that size, I'd just as soon kneel down in the water and drown myself before having to face it.

All of a sudden, every news story about alligators being released in the region came rushing back to me. It was rare and they typically caught them, but it did happen. Some asshole would go down south and buy or catch one, then bring it back up here. Unfortunately, taking care of a 500-pound reptile was a decidedly different kind of responsibility than taking care of a dog or turtle, and one that most people weren't cut out for.

Without fail, these people's alligators would end up in some pond or lake or drainage ditch. The winters were too cold for them to breed but they were at least hardy enough to survive.

I stood stock-still. The crickets and frogs screamed on, ambivalent to my plight. The water had gotten somewhat deeper from where I had originally started out and I was afraid that if I continued on in the same direction I'd hit a drop-off and plunge headfirst into whatever dark abyss lay hidden out here.

Something big slithered across my leg and in the next moment I was bolting through the swamp. My legs couldn't move fast enough as I churned the mucky bottom with my bare feet. At one point, I stepped on something sharp and it stabbed into the sole of my foot but I pushed on, my face locked in a grimace of terror.

There was no thought of direction now. Nothing but the primal instinct to flee. My head was as empty as it had been the day I was born, nothing but a combination of basic animal functions.

There was a dry crack and the scrape of bark behind me. Then another and another, getting closer fast. Whatever pursued me—if it was still the same thing—was now moving tree-to-tree.

Next thing I knew, there was a crack right above me. I halted, the water sloshing forward. Whatever was in the trees continued moving. I heard the breaking of branches and the scrape of deadwood as it hopped from branch to branch. And just for a moment, I saw it. A black shape darkening the stars as it passed beneath them. It moved on.

I t wasn't until just after sunrise that I was able to find my way back. At some point, I had blundered out of the swamp and onto dry land where I tripped through a minefield of rocks and broken branches. Just by chance, I happened upon a hill where, turning around, I spotted a thin wisp of smoke against the orange hue cast by the rising sun.

It took me what must have been another hour before I made it back to the cabin and by the time I entered the clearing surrounding the quiet structure I was freezing, scraped, torn, and utterly exhausted.

First thing I did was stumble over to the well pump and start cranking. Weariness coursed through my body and the metal pump handle was slick with morning dew. At first, there was nothing. But then, bit by bit, a trickle of black liquid began to spill out.

No, no, no, no, no.

The night had been long and taxing and by now I was so thirsty that I thought I might die if I didn't drink something immediately. Still the black water came. Mashing my eyes shut, I slowly put my lips to the stream of liquid.

The fowl substance never made it to my lips. As soon as my nose was within three inches of it I had no choice but to rear back coughing. I didn't know what had gotten into the water but it smelled like a mixture of feces and gasoline.

I had no idea what it was or what I could do to fix it. All I knew was that I needed water. We needed water. And I didn't think whatever passed for water in the nearby lake was going to cut it.

I continued to pump.

11

"Mom, where were you?" Haylie asked. I hadn't even noticed she had come outside.

She looked genuinely concerned and despite everything on my mind, it was nice to be reminded that I had a baby girl who could still worry about her mother.

"We're going into town," I said. I felt disgusting. Torn up. Mud was splattered all the way up my neck, mingling with rivulets of blood. My feet felt like they were coming apart beneath me.

"What about grandma?"

"She'll be fine by herself."

That was my hope, at least. In truth, I didn't know what would happen if she woke up and found the two of us gone. But at this point, we were out of food and out of water. I needed to go in and I didn't want to roll the dice on what would happen if I woke her up. Telling her what was going on only had about a 50/50 shot of sticking in her memory for more than ten minutes.

There were a ton of things that needed my consideration but I was tired and hungry and incredibly thirsty. Our money was limited but we had nothing in the cabin but rice, which required water to boil.

I stopped again and considered the lake, imagining what it would be like to try and boil the water. I pictured myself wading into it, letting the dried blood and muck dissolve off of my legs, the bare trees standing silent around me in their dead communion.

In the back of my head, I heard the scrape of dry bark as something moved invisibly through the branches above me. The scurry of rats. The stench of swamp. My stomach churned.

I walked inside and grabbed my purse off the counter where I had dropped it weeks ago. The only dressers were in the bedrooms, so I had been living out of my suitcase this whole time. I walked over and fumbled through some clothes; pulling out a pair of jeans, socks, and a long-sleeve button-up shirt.

I grimaced as I pulled the clothes on, every inch of skin burning where it had been nearly scraped off by the clawing fingers of the forest.

Five minutes later, we were on the road. It felt strange being behind the wheel after not using the car for so many days. I knew that the worst thing for a car was to leave it sit but something kept me from using it. Maybe it was the distractions of the surrounding area—of the day-to-day tasks. Maybe being in the vehicle was as stark a reminder as anything that I had nowhere to go.

And maybe there was a small part of me that was afraid. Afraid that if I got inside and started driving, I'd just keep on driving. Drive until I hit the ocean. Then drive some more.

The gravel crunched as it rolled away beneath us. The road looked entirely different in the daytime, so much so that I wasn't convinced I was even headed in the right direction until I rolled out onto the pavement a few minutes later and saw the dinged-up sign indicating that the town of Rockwell was 47 miles away.

I think back to that pivotal moment now. I should have seen it. We should have left. I should have gathered everyone else up and gotten out of there. Hindsight is always 20/20, I guess.

Who could have predicted what happened next? As far as I knew, I had gone sleepwalking for the first time in decades. Plagued by nightmares and grief, there was nothing there to indicate that something else was happening. Something larger. And if I had left, who's to say that my ailments wouldn't have followed? As if I had anywhere else to go.

We never like to think that there's anything bigger than ourselves. I often consider those ancient people making gods out of the wind and the rain and the seasons. I used to put that off as the unenlightened creating reasons for things that they couldn't otherwise explain. A sort of science before there was such a thing.

As I spent more time in the Norris cabin, however, there was something that I came to realize. Those people weren't Joe Blow coming home from work and thinking about the world as they drank a beer on their couch. They were a people on the edge of death. A people who had no illusion about the power they wielded over the world around them. And the thing that drove the naming of these primitive and elemental gods wasn't the need for explanation, it was the need for survival.

12

Our trip into the grocery store was a quick one. Knowing exactly what I wanted, I headed right to each item's respective aisle and filled the cart with rice, beans, bread, donuts, six pounds of hamburger, two pounds of potatoes, a brick of sliced American cheese, a gallon of vegetable oil, three of the largest bottles of dish soap I could find, and as much water as I could fit in the cart.

Haylie hustled alongside me as I drew the looks of virtually everyone in the store. My clothes had been refreshed but I imagined that I still looked as if I had just crawled out of a hole in the ground. And my god, what I must have smelled like. I had almost made it to the checkout line when I doubled back for a three-pack of deodorant.

To his credit, the guy behind the cash register acted as if nothing at all was strange. He rang me up, sending my groceries down the line to a bagger that looked like he was about 125 years old, then took my payment and said that he hoped I had a good day.

There, it's done, I thought to myself as I pushed the heavy cart out into the parking lot. I motioned for Haylie to stop and we stood on the curb drinking water and eating donuts.

I had used my card. If someone wanted to know where I was, they could probably find out. Did collection agencies do that? Did they watch people's card activity?

I doubted it. Maybe a few months from now if they somehow got law enforcement involved, but if that was a possibility then I probably still had some time.

We'll have probably frozen to death by then, so joke's on them.

The problem was, they already knew where we were. Or at least they probably did. It was possible that they had just mailed out letters to every piece of property in my family's name but that didn't sound right. Surely there was some level of confidentiality they sought to maintain.

Those were all concerns for the future though. Right now, I just wanted to get home, eat some food, clean myself up, and go to sleep.

As we drove back, Haylie finally broke her silence. "Where were you?"

I didn't know how to answer that. Eventually, I gave her some vague excuse about sleepwalking but to be honest that was the only way I could explain it to myself. I'm not sure I believed it. When I had awoken to find myself standing in that swamp I had felt transported, not like I had just walked a mile-and-a-half through the woods in my bare feet.

Feet that were really beginning to ache, now that I was thinking about it. For a moment, I considered going back and grabbing some disinfectant, but I ended up forgoing it. I was tired. I was still hungry—hungry for something that wasn't glazed in sugar.

"When are we going back home?" Haylie asked, not for the first time.

I tried to speak but something caught in my throat.

I took stock of myself. If I just let loose right now, would I be able to cry? Would something finally break inside of me and crumble apart?

I forced it down, composed myself, and said, "Not for a while, honey."

"What about school?"

"What about it?"

"I mean, am I going to go to school?"

"Maybe." In all honesty, I wasn't sure what we were going to do. Fall was already in full-swing. There were no buses that came this far out, I was pretty sure. Maybe I'd have to homeschool. It sounded hard but not impossible.

"Is Grandma going to die soon? Like Dad and Jacob?"

I was caught off guard. I started to answer about three different times, then stopped. How could I? I eventually settled on something approximating resolve.

"No."

We came upon our road and turned off, gravel crunching as the pavement disappeared. I shot a quick look in the rearview mirror and caught sight of the road sign. Rockwell 67. I blinked.

Gosh, did I just drive over an hour in each direction for bottled water?

"Yes, she is." Haylie delivered the statement with the cynicism of someone four years older than she actually was.

"No, she's not," I shot back. Then, "If she passes, we'll be there for her."

"And that's different?"

"Of course it is," I snapped. I looked down to see my hands shaking on the steering wheel.

"She's not going to get sick in the hospital like Jacob?"

"Jacob didn't get sick in the hospital," I said. And it was true. Her brother had been sick long before he went into the hospital. It was for fear of infection they wouldn't let us in to see him though. The last time I saw him, I was standing outside his room staring through the window and breathing through a light blue surgical mask.

"Susan said that she got to see her mom when she was in the hospital. They had to wear masks but—"

"Do I look like Susan," I shouted. "I'm not one of your little fucking friends."

Silence sank down between us. I shot a glance over and saw Haylie staring out at the passing scenery. The window reflected the faintest image of her face back at me. Her lips were clamped in a tight grimace, her cheeks wet and shining.

In our remaining time at the Norris cabin, she never said another word to me.

13
___

I found myself fishing alone the next day. Haylie stayed back with her grandma as I packed up the gear and wound my way through the rat-infested woods to the lake. The sky overhead was a leaden gray. The air was thick and strangely humid with only the slightest of breezes rippling across the water.

I tied new hooks onto both of the fishing poles then checked the line. It didn't immediately snap which was a good sign and kept me from kicking myself too hard for not picking up some new gear in town the previous day. I then walked around rolling logs over and stuffing grubs and other bait-like creatures into one of the small grocery bags I had brought in from the car.

After casting out the lines, I jammed the handles into the soft ground and sat down on a small patch of straw-colored grass a few feet away. The routine was familiar by now. I always had to make sure that I didn't cast too far out. Not only did I want to avoid the large fish in some of the deeper parts of the lake but I also wanted to minimize the amount of time I had to fight anything as I reeled it in.

Anything that was either too big or on the line for too long increased my chances of the line breaking.

Over the next hour, I watched the tips of the rods against the silver sky. I pulled in three bluegills and a small bass. Trying to occupy my mind, I made short work of them with a flimsy filet knife I had sheathed on my belt, rinsed the meager pieces of meat, and then folded them into another grocery bag that I had kept separate from the bait bag.

I leaned back when I was done. It was quiet, the water rippling gently in front of me like wrinkled skin. I suddenly felt the dead sitting with me. First Alina, dead from an overdose. Then Luis, leaving me with two children to raise on my own. One of those children, Jacob, would then come down with pleuropulmonary blastoma and die alone in an empty hospital room.

Three deaths that were close to me, all passing from different things. But they were all the same thing, weren't they? Illness, addiction, despair. It was all just sickness. Sickness in a broken world.

I squeezed my eyes shut and rocked my head back and forth a few times. The air around me felt suddenly sickly and cloying. The dampness hung there, suffocating me. With a huff, I stumbled back to my feet and swiped the grocery bag with the fish fillets in it from the ground.

As I was reeling in the second line I heard a big swirl of water from the snarl of weeds off to my right. I froze. Smooth waves of water rolled toward me.

My heart began to hammer inside my chest as memories from two nights ago came flooding back. The swamp. The dark. The thing in the water and the trees. In the daytime, I had felt stupid for being afraid of what was probably a beaver and some night bird but I didn't feel as stupid now.

I waited a few more seconds and then began to reel in

the second pole as fast as I could, my eyes on the weeds the whole time. There was a sudden clack and a shock of fear seized me by the neck. Panic shook my every nerve until I realized the sound was just my sinker hitting the last eye of the fishing pole. I reached out and grabbed the dangling hook, pulled it an inch or so down to the nearest eyelet, and secured it in place.

There was another swirl, this time between me and the weeds. My head snapped up just in time to see something big roll beneath the surface. Something long and grey.

I grabbed the gear and ran, even as my mind told me it was just a big fish. Even as the mechanisms of logic told me that I was overreacting. I still ran all the way back to the cabin, the tackle box jangling in my right hand, poles bobbing in my left. I didn't look back. Didn't want to look up into the trees and see...

Anything. Anything at all.

I must have been less than a hundred feet from the cabin when I first heard the wailing.

"What is it?" I asked, panicked. I was out of breath, the tips of the poles slapping against the ceiling as I forced my way through the door.

But no one needed to tell me. It was clear.

My mother was rocking on the couch emitting a noise somewhere between a moan and a yell. She was holding her face with both hands. Blood was dripping down between her fingers and even from where I was standing I could tell that it was swelling up.

"What happened?" I tried again.

Haylie was standing next to her, eyes wide and silent.

"The men. It was the men," my mother cried. "They-"

she made a sharp slashing motion with her right arm, "-hit me. They hit me with their chains and bats. They wanted the money."

"What?" Now I was confused. "What men? Who did this?"

But she just kept repeating, "The men, the men."

In all of her keening, I had neglected something in the back of my head. Something I heard. It was right there out in the open but the shock of the situation was so confusing as to push it temporarily out of focus. Gradually though, I began to realize something.

Somewhere, there was a phone ringing.

My cellphone had been turned off for weeks at this point but nevertheless, I instinctively patted down my pockets. After realizing that it wasn't my phone, I looked around, hoping the mystery would be revealed. Or at least, I was hoping that it would be revealed to be something other than what I feared.

The ringing was coming from the basement. High-pitched, oddly resembling the cries from my mother, the sound was muffled but insistent. I didn't want to believe it. Didn't want to consider what that meant. Who it could be. But I had to know, above all else, I needed answers.

"Help clean up your grandmother," I said to Haylie. And before I could see if she was obeying me or not, I rushed out of the room and through the doorway and down the steps to where the phone was sitting, still covered by the heavy box.

After hefting the box out of the way, I stared down at it. Black and ancient. Inexplicable. I reached down and lifted the handle off of its cradle and put the receiver to my ear.

"Hello," I said. I put a little more punch into the word than I had wanted but I needed it to force my way past the apprehension that was swirling around the top of my head like a clutch of buzzing flies.

No answer. Just the same steady breathing. But this time there was something in the background. Some extraneous noise that simultaneously evoked images of crashing waves and screeching train tracks.

"Leave me the fuck alone," I hurled into the mouthpiece. I knelt down and slammed the receiver back down, the innards of the machine chiming like a handful of smothered bells.

It was irrational, I know. As far as I knew, this was the first time the phone had ever rung. But stacked on top of the occurrence a few nights ago, running from the area down by the lake, and finding my mother bleeding on the couch it was all just too much.

I went back upstairs and asked Haylie what had happened but she was silent.

"Do you want this to happen again?" I asked, pointing at her grandma's bleeding face.

Her lips were sealed though and I slammed out through the door in a huff.

The air outside was so heavy I almost hunched beneath the weight of it. How was that possible? It was fall, not summer. But it felt like I was in a microwave. I shut my eyes and took a deep breath, the humidity flooding my lungs.

When I opened my eyes again, I noticed something laying on the ground. I knelt down and picked it up. A cigarette. And not just a cigarette, but one that had clearly been crushed out in the dirt for there was the imprint of a heavy foot where I had retrieved it.

Flicking the cigarette away, I stalked forward following the sets of tracks. They were big. Male. They weren't mine and they definitely weren't Haylie's or my mother's. I half-expected them to lead to a set of tire tracks in the driveway but they didn't. Instead, they led off into the woods, heading in the direction of the swamp.

I lost their tracks once they hit the brush. I stopped and looked around. Nothing was moving. Everything was silent. Nothing but the oppressive atmosphere.

"Leave us alone," I screamed. The words were almost muffled, seeming to diffuse against the wall of humidity.

I stomped back inside and for the first time, I noticed that it was just as hot inside as it was out. The cabin had a few small fans but no air conditioning. Haylie's face was slick with sweat as she dabbed my mother's cheek with a damp towel, the white tip now pink with blood.

She stepped back and handed me the towel as I approached. I took it from her and continued to clean my mother up, who was now stone-faced, her eyes staring in a blurry haze.

THAT EVENING I TOOK A QUICK WALK DOWN THE ROAD TO finally empty the mailbox. Thinking about the supposed men that had come to our cabin reminded me of the overflowing box at the end of our long gravel drive. I felt a little hesitant leaving Haylie and my mother there alone again but I figured if anyone was coming this way they'd have to come down this road first.

Halfway to the box however, I came across a black Toyota Camry parked on the side of the road. The car was tilting slightly into the ditch, one of its front tires flat. I walked around, cupping my hands against my face to peer through the windows. There were a few fast food drink cups sitting in the holders and a wadded up grease-stained paper bag behind the passenger seat but other than that the car was empty.

I stepped back and looked around. The car was clean. A little too clean. A rental most likely. It had probably hit a sharp rock as it turned onto the gravel road or maybe caught a nail on the highway. What didn't make sense though was the fact of the missing driver.

If this car belonged to the men who had assaulted my mother, then where were they? Why hadn't they come back yet? I thought about the tracks leading off into the woods. Could they still be out there? There weren't many houses nearby. If it were me, I would have forgone whatever plans I had had to pilfer money from a single mother, a little girl, and an old woman. Who cared? Stuck out here, we were their only lifeline.

I continued my walk to the mailbox, trying to make sense of the whole thing.

If they were nefarious enough to beat my mother with a fucking chain then why not steal my car? It would have been easy enough. The keys were right on the counter.

Nothing was adding up. Who had heard of people sending thugs with baseball bats to collect money? I was in debt to a lot of people but none of them were the *mob*. At least, not that I knew of.

When I reached the mailbox, I was so lost in thought that I almost missed the sign. First, I scooped a bunch of warped and pale adverts out along with a few envelopes, then I stuffed it all into the same bag I had put the live bait in.

Whatever. I didn't care.

Then it hit me. I stopped, head down in the middle of the road, straddling the two white lines, one broken and one solid. I turned and read the sign. Then I read it again. Then again and again. I stared at it, hoping for it to make sense. But it didn't.

Rockwell 153.

I couldn't remember what the exact mileage had been last time but I remembered it being just over an hour in one direction. This was over two-and-a-half. Did I end up on some other road? Did I read the sign wrong the first time?

I couldn't have read the sign wrong. Driving to the store, I had thought the drive only took about 45 minutes going just over the speed limit. It had taken longer than that but I was acutely aware of how much time it was taking on account of my exhaustion. Another minute spent in that car would have been another chance to fall asleep and drive off the road. No, I wasn't hallucinating. Something was wrong.

The problem was, I didn't know what to do about it. There wasn't exactly some road-sign manager I could ask for.

Sir, your mileage signs keep on changing. And by the way, did you know that your forest is filled with rats? Totally disgusting, and that's not the worst of it. I woke up half-naked in a swamp, my mother was beaten by some knee-breakers right out of a hard-boiled detective novel, and oh yeah—they've disappeared.

If a car had come around the corner, their driver not paying attention, I probably would have been struck and killed. I stood there in the middle of the road for what seemed like hours. Who knew? What was time anymore? Apparently, there weren't any rules to anything.

I walked back to the cabin in a fog. My feet were hurting again by the time I got back and I gingerly slipped my shoes off after plopping down on the futon. As I did, a number of Haylie's crayon drawings slid toward me as I sank into the cushion.

I closed my eyes for a moment, letting my body relax. Then I opened them back up and began flipping through the crude etchings.

Haylie had never been a particularly good artist. She was too undisciplined for something like that. Too wild and prone to heavy marks on the page and over-enunciated images. I take that back—they were almost good, in a manner of speaking. There was a certain visceral flair to them.

One drawing showed a chain striking a clay pot. There were no finer details or background images. Just the objects crashing into each other. All of them were like that. Wide open mouths with teeth that seemed to stretch outward. People being punched and slapped. Lighting. Car accidents. A wave of force and violence rendered in raw images. I flipped through them and then stopped. Something had pricked my attention but I wasn't sure what.

I slowly paged through them again, looking carefully at each one until I found it. The first time I had seen it I had written it off as a strange Christmas tree but that wasn't exactly right. The shape was there but the color and proportions weren't. The tree was brown and had no leaves or needles on it, and the star at the top was black.

Even then, it took a moment to strike home but when it did I felt a tendril of fear slide like a cold finger up the back of my neck.

I had seen it before. The tree, I mean. It was only by some vague suggestion of logic that I remembered it but there it was. Our first morning here when we had gone out for a walk to see the lake. The scrape of bark on the trees, just like my night in the swamp. But I hadn't seen anything either time.

But apparently, Haylie had. Or at least she had sensed it. The tree was right. The way the branches jutted in odd directions painted an image of someone frozen in distorted pain.

I stared for a long time at the shape on top. It could have been a star. All the other images were just as crude but it was hard to tell. Something about it felt off, though. Wrong. Maybe it was the rounded edges, but the shape seemed to imply something almost organic. Two feet, two arms, and a head. It was possible.

What it meant though, I couldn't even begin to fathom.

15

———

The last dream arrived that night, a pinprick of grace to dissolve all things.

I dreamt I was sitting in the rocking chair we had in our nursery before Luis died. I was holding Jacob, my baby boy, in my arms. It was just past 3:30 a.m. and I had been awakened by his crying. I fed him with the lights off, just a small trickle of light coming in from the bathroom down the hall.

After I had finished, he was still fussing about, making little coos and trying to roll over. I held him to my chest, sitting there in the darkness rocking gently. I felt his soft cheek against my breast, the gentle rise and fall of his little body as he dozed. The inky black space like a womb, holding infinity in the flesh.

I was rooted there. Even though sleep with an infant around is a precious commodity, I stayed there holding him against me. In that quiet hour, I had the distinct feeling that this moment would remain with me no matter what. Regardless of how he grew up and what he would become, all of the good and the bad, there would always be this. The two of us sitting here for all time.

And it struck me then that the conception of a child is an act of faith, a commitment to love in spite of all potential action and consequence.

Later, I held onto that memory like a lifeline. A way of holding his hand through the barriers of brick and glass and quarantine. I remembered it when I got the call, the telephone burning red with the Hell of separation.

After he passed, I realized that ever since that night I had known it would turn out this way. Maybe not the details, but I had known—known that the tiny body I was holding in my arms had a little heart beating inside of its chest and that when it stopped, he would be alone in a sterile hospital room without his mom.

I awoke to find my eyes already open, my face wet. The transition was so seamless that I wasn't actually sure if it had been a dream or something that I had remembered while lying there. I remained there for what must have been another 30 minutes, savoring the memory like the taste of ash and honey.

L ater that night, the phone rang again.

The first time. I stomped down the stairs and tried to yank it from the wall. The wires that were tethering it however were too strong, so I just ended up disconnecting it where they met the phone itself.

I laid back down, staring at the ceiling. I didn't know what time it was but it still felt early, probably before midnight. I tried to sleep but couldn't. I could barely even close my eyes. It wasn't until the phone rang again that I knew I had been waiting for it.

This time I walked more slowly, almost as if in a daze. If I was sleepwalking somehow, then so be it. I knew what was coming. Knew what I was about to do.

Once in the basement, I found where the phone line connected to the wall. There was a small beige plate where the wire ran through and unlike other phones I had seen, the wire continued to run in and through the wall itself rather than just plugging in. I pried the plate off with a large flat head screwdriver, revealing a tiny hole in the wood paneling.

Crouching down, I put my eye against the hole to see what I could see. The tiny light bulb dangling from the ceiling didn't illuminate much and as soon as I got too close to the hole my shadow immediately covered it. I had seen enough though. From what I could tell, the wire ran to the right.

I walked back up the stairs, quietly pulled the jeans on I had laid in a pile next to the futon a few hours ago, slipped some shoes on, and walked to the door. I had almost made it outside when I realized I had forgotten something important. Stepping back in, I retrieved the flashlight we often used to run to the outhouse after dark. I would just have to hope that no one would have to go in the next few hours.

I stepped out into the night. The hot air had been replaced by a sharp chill and the wind was blowing hard across the treetops. All around me was the sound of clacking branches and rustling leaves. I hardened my resolve and continued forward.

As I walked around the side of the house, I expected to come across something. I didn't know what but I was sure that the small circle of illumination that was being emitted from my flashlight would slide over some disgusting creature skulking around in the middle of the night. A giant rat or unimaginable lake dweller. Maybe even one of the little goblins I had dreamt about that first night. Nubby body shuffling around, its sharp spear jabbing this way and that like some confused bird with its beak in the air.

But there was nothing. I made it to the corner of the small structure and began to dig.

I came across the phone line much quicker than I had expected, only digging down about eight or nine inches. Making sure I had the right thing, I wiped the dirt away and inspected it, comparing its general width and texture to that of the one inside. They were identical.

I pulled upward on it and ripped up through the dirt and grass. I pulled again and got a few more feet of it as it rose upward from the ground. I began to walk.

Pulling the wire up, it took me far longer than it would have if I had just been strolling along. Occasionally I would come across a fallen log or root that had grown up over it and would have to bend over and dig down until I found the other side of it. But the further I went, the more certain I was of where I was heading.

I had expected it to lead in the same direction as the road but I had been wrong. Even though a part of me knew. A part of me had known ever since the night I had dreamt of the giant rat.

I stopped and took a breath, wiping my hands on my jeans. Both were thoroughly soiled with dirt at this point and my palms had started to bleed in places. I did a slow circle with the flashlight, observing the surrounding woods. I was on one of the trails. The wind had picked up around me and I felt the buzz of electricity in the air and tasted the light pang of rain.

Other than the brewing storm, I was alone. Nothing

following me that I was aware of. No rats. No imps. No men with chains. It was as if everything around me was sleeping for the first time in its life. I switched the flashlight to my right hand and began to pull on the buried wire with my left. A few more feet came up through the ground, flinging dirt in every direction.

I gave up when I hit the edge of the lake. There was a wet swish as the wire pulled up through the mud and water and then I just stood there holding it in my hand, tracing it with my eyes against the surface of the water. I tugged on it and nothing happened.

A large gust of wind blew along the shore, a sharp chill cutting into me. My feet were still a little banged up from the other night and I was tired. For the first time since my quest to find the source of the ringing telephone, I felt my determination slip. I was out here alone, at night, in this strange place that seemed to be getting darker and more dangerous by the moment.

Thunder rolled over the lake, its heavy sound grinding into me like huge pieces of gravel. I dropped the wire and turned back. Halfway between the lake and the cabin, the first drops of rain began to fall.

16

———

THE STORM CAME ON HARD. HAYLIE WAS AWAKE BY THE TIME I got back and after about thirty minutes, my mother shuffled out of her room to join us on the futon. Wind buffeted every inch of the clapboard structure, the very floorboards vibrating beneath us. Lightning flashed over and over again and I refused to turn toward the windows, afraid of what I might see peering in from outside.

At one point, a bolt of lightning hit so close that it gave the impression of a bomb going off, the flash and the bang striking in perfect unison. Immediately following that was a deep groan and wrenching of wood as some massive tree fell nearby. The subsequent impact of it hitting the earth was enough to send all of us downstairs.

Once we were in the cellar, I watched the tiny lightbulb shake overhead, the shadows of boxes dancing around us like the ethereal remnants of the damned.

Somehow, Haylie slept. We weren't down there ten minutes before I was able to pick out her soft breathing amongst the racket. She gave out a soft groan as she stirred and snuggled into my shoulder.

To my right, my mother was leaning up against a stack of boxes, her eyes open, considering.

"We're going to be ok," she said. Her voice was so soft I thought I had imagined it, then she said. "The structure is strong. It's endured a lot."

I didn't know what to say. On one hand, I wasn't convinced she was right. The cabin had certainly been through a lot, but that didn't guarantee its continued existence. On the other hand, she seemed surprisingly lucid and I didn't want to squander the moment by arguing with her.

"How are you feeling?" I asked, choosing to settle on a different topic.

"Sore," she replied and gave a weak smile. A dark bruise was settling in on the left side of her face. She shifted and groaned, raising her hand up to her side. "They got me in the ribs too."

"Who were they?"

"I don't know. They came asking for money. There was something about them though. They looked sick. Sweaty. I think something was wrong with them."

"I think something is wrong with anyone who goes around beating up old women."

She huffed a small laugh and then winced. "You'd never force an elderly woman to do something against her will, right?"

I didn't have a witty answer for that.

She shook her head. "Don't worry dear. I get it. Dealing with me like this has got to be...vexing."

She looked up at the ceiling. There was another loud crash outside, this one rattling everything in the cabin. The light dimmed and flickered, then returned to its normal glow.

"It's just so hard to get my bearings," she continued. "I can't tell where I am half the time or how I got there. It's frightening to watch your life slip through your fingers like sand being blown away. I feel like I'm losing my whole world. Like I'm losing myself."

I muttered something weak about it being ok. That we were there for her.

"This place," she was shaking her head. "It is impenetrably lonely. There's something cold about it, like sleeping too close to a thin wall in the winter. I think there's something in you that knew, something that remembered what this place really was."

"Why do you say that?" I asked. "Why would I bring you here if I knew this place was-" I grappled for the right words but came up empty.

"You can't describe it," she said, reading my thoughts. "I know you can't. I can't. There's just something here that's different. Something alien. Something that brushes up against another mode of being. It's a wild state, disconnected from the life you're used to. Some people are warped by it. But others—I imagine there are others that might thrive here."

"I doubt that," I said, speaking honestly.

"Tell me," she said. "You left him. Why?"

"I didn't leave him," the words came out in a tumble. I composed myself. "I didn't leave him. I made every—he just...I missed him. He passed when I wasn't there."

"He was your son. After Luis, I thought that-"

"Thought what?" I cut her off. I looked down at Haylie and dropped my voice. "Thought what? Thought I'd want to do something different? Experience more of that? Say what you will about Luis but I think he knew me well enough to get it over with quickly. No waiting. No prolonged hospital stays. It was a mercy, in a way."

I checked to make sure Haylie was still sleeping. The last thing I needed was for her to hear me arguing about her dead father and brother.

"You never had to deal with death up close," my mother said. "And no one was around for you when you needed them to be. I was still busy teaching at the University when Alina died. I was too up in my own head to be there for you. And your father," she threw up her arms. "Who knows where he was. But what I'm saying is, I don't think you ever learned how."

"How? How what? How to grieve? I learned how to do that just fine, no thanks to you."

"That's not what I'm saying."

"Then what?" I felt a tremor seize the bottom of my lip as that familiar ache settled into the back of my throat. "Are you saying I can't-" I made some feeble motion with my hand. "Say goodbye?" I shrugged. "Maybe you're right. Maybe I don't know how to say goodbye to someone for the last time."

I waited for the tears to come—wanted desperately for them to grip me and wrack me with sobs. But there was nothing.

"Do you know that I haven't cried in years?" I asked. "Not while awake. Not when Luis died. Not when Jacob died. All those moments that should have made me weep, but didn't. They simply cored me out like a huge drill and that empty space that should have been filled with sorrow was filled with bewilderment and horror instead. I don't know. I don't know what to do with that." I shrugged again, my face twisting involuntarily.

Then, for the last time in my life, my mother wrapped

her arms around me and pulled me close to her. I tried to say more but couldn't get the words out. No matter how hard I tried, they always stumbled up my throat and then fell apart in my mouth before they could pass through my lips.

"There was a weird thing people used to say up here," my mother said. "I heard it from tourists all the time in restaurants and gift shops in town. They'd be getting ready to leave after a long weekend and say something along the lines of '*I guess it's time to get back to the real world.*' But I think they're mistaken. I don't think that their world is the real world."

Another roll of thunder shook the cabin.

"I think this one is."

Then there was another loud crash outside and the room was plunged into darkness.

17

The sky bled. After the storm had cleared and the sun had begun to rise upon the ravaged world, I stepped out to find the endless sheet of clouds above me ripped and red and ragged as if composed of glistening viscera. The colors were so brilliant that once I had exited the doorway I stopped and stared at its slow undulations.

The air was warm too, far different than it had been the previous weeks. It was as if I had taken some detour out of autumn, transitioning sideways into some strange alternate season that had no name.

Coming to, I noticed that the circle of empty dead grass surrounding the cabin had been broken. In multiple places around the small building lay the ruin of dead trees ripped from the earth like pulled teeth. Most troubling however was the car.

One of the larger crashes in the night must have been my old 2006 Impala being pulverized. Each of the windows had been smashed, some punctured by thick branches. And right over the top of the vehicle lay a tall white pine as wide as Haylie.

There was no fixing it. The car itself was flattened like a tube of toothpaste. If the engine worked, then it was the only thing that did. And I found it hard to believe I'd make it back to town on an engine alone.

Another problem was that the road had disappeared. For all intents and purposes, the forest had swallowed it. The driveway in which the car now lay dead was so covered in brush and branches that it was virtually indistinguishable from any other part of the surrounding woodland, making the cabin feel as if it had been transplanted onto a different planet.

I ran my fingers through my hair and then walked back inside.

"Put your shoes on," I told Haylie, who was sitting on the couch. "We're going for a hike."

She hopped to her feet, excitement in her eyes. I couldn't imagine why. Every time I went for a hike, I felt like I was about to catch some disease or get abducted by Sasquatch. Her face was alight with adventure however, and in an instant, she had her shoes on and was ready to go.

Standing where the driveway should have been, I took a moment to check my compass. Ever since finding it a few weeks ago, I hadn't gone outside without it except for trips to the outhouse and my time lost in the swamp.

The needle was somewhat hesitant to point in any solid direction though, and while it seemed to be pointing generally northward, I wasn't sure I wanted to entrust my life and my daughter's life to it just yet. We had to get out and find the road though. I wanted to know how bad the blowdown was and if we'd ever be able to leave the property again.

I had been putting off thinking about winter, along with most of my other problems, but now that the option to leave had essentially been squashed I suddenly felt suffocated. We were stuck here. We only had a little food and a limited amount of water. They were all different problems than the ones we had fled from in the first place but these suddenly seemed just as insurmountable.

I thought about boiling water from the lake again. I wondered if it was safe. Technically, it *should* be safe. I was pretty convinced that boiling it would remove anything harmful but I was growing less and less confident about even the most basic elements of knowledge here.

That feeling only became worse as I kicked my way through the brush, Haylie making just as much of a ruckus behind me as she followed. I was quite sure we were right where the road should have been, but whenever I looked through the mass of debris, I couldn't see any sign of it. As far as I could tell, the ground we were walking over was just more forest floor. No gravel or beaten-down dirt. Just leaves and pine needles.

The thought was unnerving. When we came across the third tree growing in the place I thought the road should have been, we doubled back and started over. This was fruitless however, as we made the same discovery.

The road had disappeared.

I looked over at Haylie. She had sticks in her hair and her face was smudged with dirt and sap. I couldn't quite read her expression, but she seemed to be wearing the face of someone with their mind set on a singular task. She didn't look exhausted or frustrated. She looked engaged.

It wasn't a bad thing, I figured. She still wasn't speaking but she didn't seem to outwardly hate me. Her silence was beginning to feel less and less like an act of rebellion and more like some sort of psychological barrier. This didn't bode too well for us, as we didn't exactly have top-of-the-line mental healthcare out in the sticks.

I tried to refocus my mind. I felt exhausted and not just because of my lack of sleep the previous night. Everything was mounting up. We had come here because we had nowhere else to go and now it seemed we were stuck in some perverse twilight of being forced to leave while also being wholly unable to.

We slowly made our way back to the cabin, stepping over logs and getting scraped by a million wooden fingers as we traversed the apocalyptic landscape. The sky's bloody hue was red as ever, even having darkened somewhat. I took a deep breath and tasted the air. Wet. The smell of sodden wood. The pungent smell of turned earth.

I prayed the sky wouldn't dump another storm on us.

When we got back, my mother was up and sitting on the futon. I tried talking a little bit but it seemed her state had degraded once again. Despite the topics, I was glad to have had a lucid conversation with her the previous night. At this point, I had no idea how many of those we had left in us.

I made a simple meal of rice and beans. Turning on the stovetop reminded me that the gas and electric bills were probably due. I had briefly considered hooking them up to my bank account and letting them drain the last of whatever was left in there but had instead opted to use the rest of our money on food. I still felt it was the right choice. It just meant we'd be eating dinner by candlelight here pretty soon.

When everyone was done eating, I asked Haylie if she could wash the dishes, reminding her multiple times that we had a limited amount of water and that she should only use what she needed. Even as I said the words, I tried to dissect my own line of thinking.

Was I really using precious water to do dishes? Did I not think we were in as bad of trouble as we were? Had I resigned myself to eventually boiling snow and lake water?

I wasn't sure. If I was being honest with myself, I would have said that having Haylie use some of our very precious drinking water for dishes was just another example of me not wanting to acknowledge a problem.

In the fatalistic haze of someone who knows they're doing something wrong but continues to do it anyway, I found myself standing there, waiting to tell Haylie to stop. To just wipe the dishes down. But of course, I didn't.

Jesus, why was I getting so hung up on dishes?

I stumbled out the door without another word. I didn't know where I was going or what I was going to do about our predicament. I felt the wheel of options spinning in my head until it slowed and that imaginary needle landed on my answer.

Check the road again.

I shook my head, trying to clear my thoughts. They were beginning to feel loose and disconnected, as if I hadn't slept for a great while. I breathed in slowly and then exhaled, looking at nothing. My thoughts aligned into something coherent and then I set out once again to find the road that no longer existed.

18

———

As I HIKED THROUGH THE DENSE UNDERBRUSH, BRANCHES slapping me in the face without concern, I felt the haze I had been under back at the cabin begin to lift off of me. The air was warm but not dense. The clouds overhead were still dark and sluggish but lacked any sense of malevolence. The more and more I walked, the closer I felt I had come to the surface of something. It was as if I had awoken to find myself at the bottom of some deep pond and was steadily forcing my way up toward the open air.

In a way I was, because moments later, the woods suddenly broke apart before me, revealing the highway where our mailbox was located. I took a moment to look up and down the empty stretch of asphalt, noticing it looked a little more worn than usual. This was likely due in no small part to the storm, as the shoulder was littered with fallen trees and broken branches.

I turned to my left and squinted. Something about the road felt wrong. I seemed to remember being able to look down it for a while before my line of sight was rounded off by a curve. But now there was no curve. Now it was just straight as far as the eye could see.

I blinked. Where had I come out? I must have been further off course than I had thought.

Suddenly remembering the compass in my pocket, I reached in and pulled it out. I flipped up the top and stared down at it.

The needle was jerking this way and that, occasionally doing four or five full rotations before coming to rest for a second and then starting all over again. It was never the same pattern. Sometimes it would spin so many times I couldn't count, while others it just did a single half-turn and then slowly retracted back into its original position.

I shook it, not sure if that would make it better or worse. Neither, apparently. I sighed and stuffed it back into my pocket.

That's when I caught sight of the road sign. It was far off in the distance and barely readable but I could tell something was wrong. I began to walk toward it, eventually breaking into a run.

I stopped at a point about ten feet away, hands on my knees as I tried to catch my breath. My feet hurt and I wondered if I had done some sort of long-term damage to them the night I had run through the swamp in bare feet. The wounds had mostly healed but ever since then, they had been constantly sore.

I stared down at the asphalt. Now that I was here, I didn't want to look up. After a few seconds, I finally forced my face upward.

Rockwell 1,347,986.

Was this a joke? Did someone have access to the necessary materials a prank like this might require? What, a few stencils and very specific shades of paint?

I turned back to the road. The gravel turnoff was gone, completely swallowed by the forest. For a moment, I thought it was possible that I might never get back to Haylie and my mother. That my entry would be barred forever now that I had broken through the barrier of the woods and out onto the road. The road that seemed to retain the quality of some sort of landmark or anchor. Something real.

But if it was real then the sign was real. And if the sign was real...

I pressed my fists into my eyes, stars flaring behind my lids. I opened them up as the world rematerialized before me.

Rockwell 3,698,542.

I let out a bark of laughter, then turned on my heel and plowed back into the forest.

Anger and frustration burned in me and pushed me forward. What was happening? Was this something in my mind? Maybe something related to my mother? What if she didn't actually have dementia but some sort of misdiagnosed illness of the brain? One that was contagious and that I had caught?

I hoped not. If it were true, then it was likely I'd never know. I had never really grappled with what it was like to have your mind slowly degrade inside your head. As far as my mother was concerned, I only saw it from the outside. It was a gradual change that I could assess while still being rooted to reality. But for her, who knew what it was like?

What was it she had said the night before? About the tourists thinking that their jobs and restaurants and suburban homes were the real world? How they had it exactly backward? Their world was the fantasy. Theirs was the dream.

The sky had become even darker. When I tried to make out the way ahead I could only see about ten to fifteen feet in front of me before the snarl of bracken dissolved into blackness. It should have only been around noon but the day seemed to have adopted the quality of some sort of perpetual twilight.

As I walked aimlessly on, the barrage of breaking limbs and branches was so loud that I barely noticed the noise rising up behind me. And then, even when I did, it was hard to make out what it was. If I had to describe it, I would have said that it sounded something like a waterfall, which wasn't actually all that inaccurate.

I stopped, feeling an almost irresistible urge to take cover. It wouldn't have helped.

In a matter of seconds, what could only be described as a wall of water raked its way through the forest, baptizing and blinding everything in its wake. It hit me like a car, sending me sprawling. I felt something stab into my upper thigh and then once again just below my left eye socket.

Blood and water clouded my vision. I blinked and rubbed my eyes until the world slowly came back together. The wall of water was gone, having raced forward. I tried to make sense of what had just happened.

I was laying on the ground, the blunt knob of a fallen log digging into my leg. I groaned as I staggered to my feet. After taking a moment to check my wounds and make sure they didn't need immediate attention, I began to walk again.

The forest had been transformed. The deadwood that had been piled in heaps for miles had been swept away to reveal a rich and earthy forest floor. The trees looked different as well. They weren't just taller and wider but seemed to have some ineffable quality of age to them, as if I weren't looking at trees but the souls of trees.

Something squawked not too far away and I wrapped my arms around my chest. Every move I made felt suddenly intrusive. I didn't want to talk. Didn't want to make a sound. If I could have, I would have folded into myself until there was nothing left but a single peering eyeball set snuggly within the hole of a hollowed-out tree trunk.

I looked up at the sky to assess the weather and saw that it had turned into the darkest shade of gold that could still be identified as such. The clouds had either blown away or flattened themselves into a singular smooth blanket that stretched out endlessly overhead.

Every sense available to me indicated that I was in a different place than I had been moments before. I could see better yet it was somehow darker. It smelled like moss and damp soil with a pungent undercurrent of something sour running through it. I heard things, felt things, tasted things near me that I hadn't perceived before. I would have thought I was in a different place entirely if I hadn't have stumbled across the cabin a few minutes later.

When I looked at the small simply-built structure, I had a hard time telling if anything about it had changed. It was the same shape and color but the area around it had shifted so radically that any point of reference I had previously had to compare it to was now gone.

The circle of dead grass around it had completely vanished. Huge green weeds now stretched up past my waist. Everything seemed larger. Wilder. I walked up the steps and opened the door.

Inside, my mother was sitting on the futon with her arms wrapped around her knees, stringy grey hair hanging down to evoke the image of some great white willow. I could hear some indistinct muttering coming from her and I strode hurriedly forward.

"Mom, where's Haylie?" I said, but she didn't respond. She just kept rocking and muttering. "Mom," I tried again.

After she failed to respond for a second time, I leaned down and placed my ear about three inches from her barely moving lips.

"It is open. It is open. It is open." She was suddenly yelling and flying at me, nails scratching. I slapped at her and pushed her away, almost falling to the floor in the process. A few of her blows had landed but she had missed the eyes.

I regained my balance and held my arms out in front of me.

"Stop!"

"It is open, it is open, it is open, it is open." Her eyes were darting wildly around the room as if she were trying to track the progress of a million wayward hornets at once.

"What is open?" But even as I said the words, I felt something clench inside my chest.

"Haylie," I squeaked out, running to the basement door. I flung it open and pounded down the steps. I had turned the lights on enough times by now to know exactly where the string was located and I reached up and tugged it and the light clicked on and I saw.

It was open. The short little door that had been stuck and barricaded with boxes was now standing wide open, the boxes pushed away. I felt an inexplicably deep aversion to going near it but I forced my feet to move.

"Haylie," I called out. The words strained in my throat. I tried again. "Haylie."

Nothing. No sound. No running footsteps. Only a deep

and pregnant silence. I must have stood there for five minutes, the quiet smothering me like a heavy pillow.

Even as I walked away, I felt the silence. The pressure. It was as if I was trying to walk around underwater. There was no noise as I marched up the stairs and nothing to indicate my opening of the door as I stepped back into the main room above.

It was this deep sense of unreality that allowed the shock of what I saw next to hit me in small increments rather than overwhelming me all at once.

My mother had had her face removed. White flecks of bone poked through the shiny gore that was the front half of her head. Her body was arched and suspended as if on invisible wires attached to her hips. The sightless gaze of her blank eyes stared at me upside down, her head lolling backward. Her ribs jutted up out of her abdomen like some horrific copse of trees. They were pink and wet with blood.

I was so shocked by the scene that I must have missed the first few ripples of movement. But as I stared, I gradually saw that the ceiling above me was black. And not just black, but textured like a mass of swarming beetles.

Then one of the tiny shapes fluttered and I realized that they weren't beetles, they were blackbirds. I involuntarily shrank back and as I did they exploded into motion. Squawking and diving and pecking, they drove me from the cabin. Their talons were like the scratching of the forest branches and drew twice as much blood.

I stumbled sideways down the porch steps, the birds evaporating into the darkness. My breath took a long time coming back, my ribs aching from where they had hit the steps as I fell.

My daughter was missing. My mother was dead. As soon as I had enough air in my lungs to manage it, I began to cry.

The tears poured out of me as I wracked with huge sobs, twin rivers of snot running down my face. I wept like a runner in a marathon. Like a boxer pouring their entire body into a desperate fight. I wept like a satellite re-entering the Earth's atmosphere, pieces of me ripping apart as I plummeted. And as I did, I felt my throat finally loosen and relax, the tension being squeezed out of it like acid.

19

———

"Haylie!" I called out with reckless abandon as I walked through the woods. The shadows melted and merged around me, the darkness warring with the scant light of which I could not find the source. At first, it appeared as if it was coming from somewhere up above, but when I tilted my head back to look at the sky all I could see was darkness.

I called out my daughter's name again and was answered by the unnerving grumble of some far-off animal. I continued to shout.

I tried to make sense of all I had seen in the last hour. The road sign, the door, my mother in her ravaged state. They flashed before me like images in a dream, strung together with vague feelings of terror and abandonment.

Feeling as if my body had been filled with some numbing agent, I walked on. The sounds around me became stranger and stranger, like a word said too many times. I ceased to understand them. Everything was simultaneously a warning and a triviality. An existential threat to a pointless existence.

Everything seemed muffled and distant. That was, until a thicket of brush began to rustle to my right. I felt the word "Haylie" rise in my throat but the ghost of caution lingered and kept me silent.

All of a sudden, a man in a torn business suit erupted from the undergrowth. He was tall and thin, the bent pair of glasses sitting on his crooked nose missing both lenses. He had scrapes up and down his face and neck and hands and his white collared shirt was torn and stained in several places.

I stumbled back, unable to process what was happening. He seemed almost not to have noticed me. He looked my way, looked back in the opposite direction, and then back at me. His eyes made contact with mine and I sat there shocked into stillness and silence. I absentmindedly noted that we probably looked quite the same, what with our haggard appearance.

"You gotta help me," he said, though his eyes said something else. They seemed to be hesitant, as if I weren't really there. Like he was speaking into the answering machine of a phone number he suspected was wrong.

"Wh-what-where...who are you?" I managed to force out.

But before I had finished asking the question, I watched him transform before my eyes. Not physically, but something inside of him. His heart. His very mind.

A cruel edge crept into his eyes and sharpened his grin. His body slackened and became a little more at ease with the situation.

"Well, well," he said. He now seemed to have a bad East Coast accent. "We've been looking for you, missy. Seems you got some bills to pay."

He reached down and pulled off his belt. And in the next

moment, the piece of leather was a heavy chain. He folded it a few times and jangled it.

"Was hoping you'd get the message, or can't your pour momma speak too good after we broke her jaw?"

Then, just as fast as he had transformed, he switched back. The chain slid from his hands, falling to the forest floor as a black leather belt. A strange, befuddled look swept over his face. But before I could react, his eyes refocused on something over my shoulder and widened.

I didn't have enough time to realize what was happening. To turn around. Before I knew it, something long and elastic seemed to fly past me and hit him in the face. I threw myself to the side, trying to steer clear of whatever was behind me. My ribs thrummed with fire. I clenched my eyes shut and felt hot tears squeezing out of them, all while a muffled screaming permeated the background.

I opened my eyes just in time to see the long elastic thing retract. A good chunk of flesh and one of the man's eyeballs came with it, the optical nerve being stretched tight and then breaking with a loud snap.

The man fell to his knees, wailing like my mother had the first night we had arrived. He must have sat there for a good couple of seconds, half of his face gone, screaming at the whole of reality without discrimination. But by this time I had already whirled to stare at his attacker.

Sitting crouched on all fours was some giant frog-like amphibian. Its eyes blazed with the stars of galaxies unknown to humanity, a pair of thin antennae bobbing on its head. There was a light sucking sound as it breathed in and out, its bulbous belly seeming to expand and deflate.

I felt a rush of air as its mouth shot open for a second time and before I could turn to see what it had latched onto, the wounded man's entire body came hurtling past me and was sucked whole into the frog's gaping mouth. The amphibious lips closed and there was a loud crunch as numerous bones were compacted. The frog stared blankly at me, a single human leg sticking up and out of its mouth as if it were the wing of a dragonfly.

My own legs were moving, the bones gelatinous with fear. I was running and sobbing as I threw myself into the darkness. The trees behind me rustled and shook as the sound of something heavy moved through them.

There was a dense thicket of brush ahead of me and I was just about to dive headfirst into it when it started to shudder. My feet skidded to a halt, just as the frog leaped to a space off to my right. My mind told me to go left but I was interrupted by a human shape emerging from the thicket.

It was another man, this one a little shorter and thicker around the midsection but wearing similar clothing to the other one. His face was so terror-stricken that he seemed intent on continuing his path forward, even if it was through me.

Out of the corner of my eye, the massive frog did something so strange and horrific that, for the first time in this telling, I hesitate to describe it.

As best as I could tell, it stood upright on its powerful back legs and let out a high-pitched chirp. Then it raised its stubby arms to the sky, cartwheeled left toward me, clapped its hands together so that they were aiming directly at the incoming man, and quickly separated them. As the hands were separated, so was the man.

A loud crack reverberated through the air as his skeleton split in two, the momentum of his flight propelling his internal organs forward where they hit me full in the face and chest. The wet pieces slowly slid off of me and fell to the ground with a heavy splat.

It was like being punched by a soft wet fist soaked in blood.

All of this was something that I had to put together afterward. At the time, all I saw was the body of a man suddenly fly apart into two pieces as my entire world turned red. I stood there, shocked into absolute silence. I tasted the tang of copper from the blood in my mouth, smelled the stink of a gastrointestinal tract being exposed to the open air.

I tried to scream but I couldn't. Just like my missing daughter, the words had been knocked out of me.

20

———

I RIPPED THROUGH THE WOODS, MY LEGS BURNING WITH THE prolonged effort of simply carrying my body from one horror to the next. I was tired. As tired as I had ever been. I had someone else's blood and gristle stuck to me—seeping into my pores—like heavy summer rain.

My knees gave out beneath me and I fell to the ground and vomited. Not much came up but my body still heaved. I spat the mixture of blood and bile out. All words were gone. There was nothing now. Nothing with which I could articulate the world around me. I sat there in the sheer unquantifiable horror of it.

Slowly, my mind began to right itself. The shock wore off by degrees, if not completely. My body was still my body. My mind was my mind and my heart was my heart. I grasped hold of this idea like a raft in a raging sea.

I don't know what happened next. I may have slept there. In all likelihood, I passed out. But the next thing I knew, I was waking up to a thick and natural silence. The world was quiet.

Looking around, I realized that I had fallen asleep near

the lake. Like everything else, it looked different. The sky was almost totally dark, permeating my surroundings with a deep blue. The lake itself seemed wider than it had been. The weeds were taller and wilder and a light layer of fog lay suspended over the water like smoke. The place looked so different that I wouldn't have recognized it if it weren't for what was lying at my feet.

The half-buried telephone line. It lay there filthy and rumpled from my having ripped it up out of the ground. The straight arrow of turned-up soil leading right down to the water's edge.

A dull light flared off to my left and for a moment I thought of the dim basement light at the cabin. I didn't want to go back there. To see the open door. To see my mother in her mutilated state. I felt a lump tighten in my throat as the thoughts came unbidden.

But as I turned toward the light, I saw that it was a firefly. Fat and silent, the thing blinked off and then on again. Then there was another not far from the first. All of a sudden, I was surrounded by the blinking bugs, and what they illuminated pierced me with hope.

It was Haylie. Or at least, another girl that looked like her from behind. It had to be though, it had to.

I walked along the shore to the patch of weeds where she was standing, her little hand darting out to try and catch the flashing insects. I was hesitant. After all I had seen I had ceased to trust what was in front of me, ceased to believe that I understood a single thing about the world in which I lived. I placed my hand on her shoulder.

She turned her head and I shrank back. I should have been ready for it, but I wasn't. Even if someone had told me what to expect, I still would have felt that plummeting sense of shock.

She had my mother's face. Worn and wrinkled and drooping, she stared back with old eyes. There was a spark of something in them though, something knowing and ageless. A reflection of Haylie before her father had died. A reflection of me before I had lost my sister. Maybe even my mother when she had been a child. The spark still encapsulated those events but ceased to bear them as wounds. It was as if I was peering into the healed soul of everyone I had ever loved, reconciled to some timeless and renewing spirit.

I felt myself soften. I didn't know who was in front of me but as a mother, I understood that my daughter was in there somewhere, safe and unafraid. She turned back around and began to chase the inordinately large fireflies again.

That was when I took a closer look at one of the bugs as it drifted by me. Its body didn't look like any bug I had ever seen. There were aspects of it that seemed familiar but that I didn't immediately recognize. Slowly, it dawned on me.

They weren't bugs. They were cities.

Like a view from a passenger jet window as it begins its descent, each of the glowing lights was not an insect, but a major city. Hundreds of intricate buildings, each varying in degrees of height and size and color. All clustered together in the name of efficiency.

One blinked on for a few seconds and then blinked back off again.

My sense of wonder was suddenly shattered as something long and black shot out of the dark and snatched one of the tiny lights out of the air. I backed hurriedly away, tugging Haylie with me. I watched the shape of the giant frog materialize out of the dark, those glowing eyes staring awkwardly upward in slightly different directions.

Haylie dashed forward, slipping out of my hands. I ran

to catch up to her but before I could she was wrapping her arms around the monster. It leaned back and let out a deep chirping sound that reverberated through the wood and across the lake.

It clicked for me then. The frog. The shape. The bulbous middle and rounded limbs like a star. That first day we had been here, Haylie had seen it perched on the dead tree. She had seen it and I hadn't.

That didn't keep me from trying to tug her away though. I forced my way in and attempted to pry her off of the slick body. A cold burst of fear forked through me like lightning. I tried not to look up into the thing's face. I could smell it. Slightly damp and musty. Alien.

The frog placed a rubbery hand on my shoulder and gently pushed me. I wriggled away in revulsion but instantly came back, grabbing Haylie's arm. I tried to speak to her, to tell her to get away, but I couldn't. It seemed I had lost my ability to speak.

No need. Haylie stepped away of her own volition and looked at me. The sight of my mother's face tied an uncomfortable knot in my stomach.

Reaching behind its back, the frog produced an odd-shaped oval that appeared to be made out of some sort of glass. It then shot out its lightning-fast tongue and sucked in another "firefly." This time, however, it brought the glass vessel to its lips and carefully spat the little light into it. The intensity of the bug's illumination increased tenfold, lighting up the forest and reeds at the edge of the lake.

Further off into the forest, another one of the odd lantern-like objects lit up, this one hanging from a tree. Then another one beyond it did the same. One by one, I watched as a huge section of the forest became illuminated by the strange lights, each of them occasionally blinking off and then back on again.

By the light of each lantern, I saw that the trees were not just trees but had some sort of doors and windows carved into them. Occasionally, one of them would have some other sort of artificial protrusion upon which one might sit or relax out in the open. Between each of the dwelling structures hung long and dangling vines, spaced just close enough that a small child might be able to swing from one to the other.

I peered closely at the firefly that the frog had captured and noticed that it wasn't just one city in there but a great multitude of them passing in sequence. Each time one of them blinked out and went dark, a new one would take its place.

A great number of the fireflies were still loose and wild and Haylie ran off into a swarm of them, hopping silently as she tried to catch them. I watched as she poked her little pink tongue out, trying to catch one but failing. The bugs undulated in the air as she danced throughout their midst, moving steadily further into the woods.

I moved to follow her but was stopped by the giant frog. My fear of the creature had yet to totally subside but it had made no move so far to harm either me or my daughter. It stood there with its snub face pointing at me, antennas bobbing in the air.

With a slow, almost casual movement, it bent over to the ground and lifted something up. It took me a moment to understand, but then I got it. It was holding the phone line. The same line that had run from the cabin and on into the water.

The frog gestured for me to take it, raising it up and bobbing its head. I caught a flash of its brilliant eyes, the sheen of the lantern in its other hand flaring briefly on its lips.

Hesitantly, I reached out and grasped the wire. It was cold and grimy with dirt but as I began to pull on it, I saw that it led me straight through the middle of the woods. Step-by-step, I began to follow it, pulling myself along as a guiding line.

The frog turned and followed at my side and as we walked, Haylie danced in and around us, still trying to catch the fireflies. Eventually, she succeeded and when she turned to smile at me, her lips and teeth were bright with a glowing golden slime.

As we walked, I began to notice small movements in the trees. Creatures that were unlike the frog but thankfully unlike the rats as well. They were squat little things, pointy ears jutting asymmetrically up into the air like ill-placed party hats. I also began to notice a sound, a sort of chittering noise that I couldn't understand, but bore the patterns of speech.

The further I walked, the more distinct it became. Then gradually, it all began to blend together into a sort of song. It was accompanied by the soft wind whistling through the branches and the rhythmic chirp of night insects. The strange melody at the center never dipped or crescendoed but seemed to turn back in on itself in a sort of constant cycle.

That's when things began to look familiar. Trees and bushes and tiny houses that had all looked similar at the beginning were now unique and recognizable. So much so that they almost became a comfort, a point of reference. They passed by again and again but I never seemed to reach the cabin to which I was sure I was heading.

As it turned out, however, I would never see the cabin

again. Instead, there was a point where the trees began to thin. The canopy opened up overhead and the thick forest floor transformed into a sort of black sand. A boggy tang became palpable in the air and before I knew it I was standing before another lake, this one similar to the one I had left but much wider and darker. Living trees stretched up out of the water and blotted out any semblance of the sky above, making it appear as if I was in some sort of cave.

I stopped at the shoreline. The water was absolute glass. Impenetrable darkness.

My daughter came up beside me and stood to my left, the frog at my right.

Without warning, Haylie pranced forward and dove into the black water. Silver ripples cruised over the surface. The frog stepped forward, walking until it was submerged up to the waist. It looked back at me.

I felt the wire in my hands. I pulled on it. The line was firm. I began to walk.

The water was cool, slipping gently up my legs as I proceeded slowly into the lake. Haylie hadn't come up yet and I began to have my doubts. I looked up into the frog's eyes and felt an almost velvety calm slide over me. I continued on.

The bottom didn't feel like anything but also didn't feel like nothing. It was indescribable. My sore feet relaxed and began to prickle with numbness, like the nerves were being gently pulled apart. Soon, my body seemed to be moving forward of its own volition, my mind floating out into the ether as if I was stepping into outer space. The stars in the frog's eyes swirled as it walked with me.

The water slid over my mouth and filled my nostrils. I had a moment of hesitation as it reached my eyes, then in the next moment, I was completely submerged.

EPILOGUE

THIS STORY MAY APPEAR AS A LINE. A SEQUENTIAL TELLING from left-to-right, top-to-bottom. But it is not. Every story has a million stories in it and a single life is not a straight line. Each life is an unknowable number of wayward threads colliding infinitely with each other. One day we will endure that final collision. The end of our thread. Our fate. We will collide with an impassable barrier and all of the things we were connected to will shift like the ground beneath our feet.

I have yet to conjure my words in a way that one might fully understand them but you, the reader, have done half of the communicative work from where you sit on your side of the Veil of Rain.

This story began in the Cold Water Forest but I don't think I am there anymore. This place is different than anywhere I have ever been but the frog guides me. I have come to suspect that the plot of land the old Norris cabin sits on is like a heavy stone, slowly sinking into that deep and unknowable swamp. It is a doorway, a secret path into that strange and liminal season.

I cannot say if I am dead or not. Every death is simultaneously a wound and a healing and at the death of all things, all things will be healed. Even death itself. But I am not there yet.

There is a black light around me. A seeing that is past my eyes and a feeling that has elevated my heart. I traverse the void with the telephone wire in my hand, following it right up to a black telephone sitting upon a wooden altar. I pick up the receiver and place it to my ear.

I am connected and listening. I fall to my knees and weep.

THE END

The Omen Tree

ALSO BY FREDRICK NILES

Ash Above, Snow Below

ABOUT THE AUTHOR

Fredrick Niles is the author of *Ash Above, Snow Below* and *The Omen Tree*. He lives in St. Paul, Minnesota where he writes fiction and plays music. In his free time he rants about movies, lurks in bookstores, and practices introversion with his wife.

facebook.com/fredrricknilesauthor

instagram.com/fredrickniles_author